CORVUS and ME
THE INDIGENOUS SPIRIT

Enjoy!

Joëlle Hübner-McLean
2018!

Joëlle Hübner-McLean

CORVUS AND ME: THE INDIGENOUS SPIRIT
by
Joëlle Hübner-McLean
Copyright © Joëlle Hübner-McLean 2017
Cover Design © Jana Rade 2017
Published by Howling Wolf
(An Imprint of Ravenswood Publishing)

HOWLING WOLF

Ravenswood Publishing
1275 Baptist Chapel Rd.
Autryville, NC 28318
http://www.ravenswoodpublishing.com

Printed in the U.S.A.

ISBN-13: 978-1974026548
ISBN-10: 197402654X

This is for my Maman, Papa and younger sister.

Chapter One

"**M**ama! Mama! Where are you?" The, skinny, five year old girl walked in circles, crying.

The strange men were burning down her village. People screaming, sobbing and dying. The voyageurs that had picked up the furs watched from a distance as the stricken smallpox Ojibwa people perished in front of their eyes on the peninsula. Her family, who had always loved her, was not responding. Fear set in as she tried to find them, but the flames were too high and her skin began to sear from the heat. Wandering aimlessly, crying, wiping her stinging tears from her face, she tried calling once more.

"Please, Mama, answer me! Where are you?" she screamed with all her might. She sat by the burning corpse. "Where are you?" she whimpered. Her strength gone, gasping and wheezing, she lay down beside the dead body and knew her life would soon be over. Her favorite sky blue wool dress, embroidered with white beads and small shells, was ruined. It like, the white ribbon wrapped around her

1

braided, black, silky hair, and her new moccasins were covered in ash.

Afraid, hopeless and shattered, the young native girl struggled to breathe and see. It was not until that moment she felt something tugging her from the rubble, away from the flames. As she tried to open her sore eyes, she thought she saw a grey wolf, or the spirit of a wolf, but passed out without knowing for sure.

****

You are always there for me. Twelve year old Janine walked on a pathway she was familiar with. When she found a black crow's feather, she looked around to see if she could find Corvus: he was nowhere to be found, so she kept the feather. She knew, once again, her journey was make-believe, another dimension where she would soon meet up with her close friends: Right Whisper, the talking mirror extracted from a maple tree, and Corvus, the crow.

It would not be long now before another mission was at stake but why was she standing in her favorite summer camp in the early sixty's, where her parents and sister used to spend their holidays? There were no children to be seen. Janine knew that Right Whisper would turn up soon and explain what had happened to her this time.

Situated close to the lake stood a wooden two-storey building with wide picture windows; she knew there were, several bedrooms at the top and a general store at the bottom. Janine opened the mahogany door gently and walked into the building. The familiar scent filled the air from the different candies to the marina gear the owner had in stock. Then something caught her eye. A large shadow moved behind the counter before it disappeared.

"Who's there!" Janine nervously shouted as she glanced around and heard nothing more. "Is anybody there? You're scaring me! Show yourself!" Her heart pounded, but she was determined to find out who the intruder was. She slowly walked to the stairs behind the counter and, little by little pulled herself up the steps, cautiously looking for the mysterious shadow. Her chest tightened and she, wheezed as she leaned against the wall to catch her breath. When that

2

didn't work, she bent over, her hands clutching her knees as she struggled to breathe. Her asthma was acting up. She needed to rest for a few minutes.

"Why…why are…you hiding?" she asked with difficulty. "Here…I… come…" She peered quickly into a large bedroom on the right, but saw nothing, before she slowly made her way to the large room on the other side. No one.

"I'm sure I saw something," she said in a soft voice. With her breathing under control, she walked toward the large bedroom that had once been occupied by the hired help. She could almost see them in her mind, the lost and abandoned women who had worked here. Some of them mentally challenged, others simply forgotten by life. These detached women had been institutionalized throughout the year, but during the summer season, the owner of this camp, would hire the women. They would do small jobs like cleaning the adjoining cabins and making dinner for the guests who rented the cabins for the weekends or week. The women would stay two months, and, if they behaved, chances were good that they'd come back for the next summer season.

But this time, no one was present. "Huh. Where are they?" Janine asked the empty room before she turned and followed her path back out of the building. She gazed around the front of the building at the expanse of the property and looked for her friends or the strange shadow, but there was no sign of anyone being there.

Standing on the dock half an hour later, Janine enjoyed the cool, late spring air, mesmerized by the water flapping against the rocks close by. She peered into the murky depths as she searched for snapping turtles, but found none. Suddenly, she felt a presence eyeing her. Perched on a cedar tree, a shiny black crow cawed to get her attention, and as she turned around, there stood Corvus.

"Corvus," said Janine. "You left a feather in the pathway over there and that is why I knew you would show up sooner or later. By the way, you did not see something strange, did you?"

"Nope. Are you ready for another journey?" Corvus asked as he tilted his shiny, black, plumy head. "But first we must see Right

Whisper so that she can tell us where to go," he finished with a guttural sound.

"Where is she? Do you know?" asked Janine as she studied the crow carefully. "And besides, how did you keep a mirror from melting since I found her in the wintertime?"

"I carried her in a small box, and kept her in very cold water. She should be fine for a little while, if we keep her in a cool place. Or on ice," Corvus cawed.

"Yeah, right. Where do we get ice? And how come you can fit her in a small box?"

"Magic." He answered simply. "You know that general store located at the Native reserve about two miles west from here? They keep the blocks of ice in sawdust in the basement."

"Oh, yeah, I remember. That is a good idea, but how will we carry her without melting throughout our trip? Besides, I thought you would know about all these missions before Right Whisper does, since you see J. Regia most of the time. You know, the smart tree that sends you off on these tours."

"That's true, but with Right Whisper, she can give you the whole story while I generally give you the Reader's Digest version."

"That is for sure. Short and to the point. My Maman liked those small paperback books called, 'Selection' in French, and she read the non-fiction stories all the time. I remember because, I found them on her dresser in my parents' bedroom when I was cleaning the house."

"Well then, you know that I am a crow with very few caws." Janine wrinkled her forehead at the crow's attempt at humor.

"To answer your other question about how to keep Right Whisper from melting, I have already collected small pieces of broken ice from the basement of the general store. I have paced it, with some sawdust, into a rawhide pouch so the moisture will stay."

"Yes, but the last two times she changed from a piece of ice to a hard rubbery form."

"Right, but it was still cool then. Not warm weather like we have now," said the crow.

"Oh. I see. Well then, a rawhide pouch made out of deer or moose hide is great for safekeeping? Are they strong enough?" Janine asked.

4

"They sure are; if tanned right. The kind of deerskin bags you need are about six inches by seven inches with a stitched flap. It is quite sturdy and it weighs almost nothing." He handed her a pouch. "Here you go. I found an old pouch laying on the ground as I made my way out of the basement window. You can tie around your waist, and you would not have to worry about losing it while we are on our trek. It will be big enough for Right Whisper."

"You just happened to find this pouch laying on the ground." Janine examined it carefully for defects.

"Yup! Lucky, eh?" said the crow.

"Let's hope it works. So anyway, what happened to me this time? Did I trip and hit my head or something like that?" Janine chuckled, shaking her head as she attached the small pouch around her waist.

"Right Whisper will show and discuss it with you when you see her. And, by the way, I like your duds," he told her.

Chuckling to herself, she shook her head again, "Oh these old track pants were given to me by my parents' friends. Their kids are the same age as my sister and I." Corvus motioned Janine to move on as to the location of where Right Whisper was placed.

"Nice to see you again this fine afternoon, Janine." She jumped in surprise, not realizing Right Whisper was lying against a rock as water cascaded over the rock to keep her cool. "Did I scare you?" Right Whisper asked softly.

"Yeah."

"I tend to do that sometimes. Love the white ribbon in your hair and beaded necklace."

"Good afternoon to you too, and thank you. That was my mother's idea." Janine showed off her bow. "But the necklace was mine. She has always tied ribbons in our hair one way or another, for both my sister and I. See my new necklace I bought it at the reservation store?"

"Lovely. Still a slim young lady I see. What do you have in your hand?" Right Whisper asked.

"Oh, this!" Janine looked at the feather she was holding. "I think it belongs to Corvus." She placed the black feather securely into her

5

ponytail and turned around slowly for Right Whisper and Corvus to see. "How do I look?"

"Lovely, simply lovely. Doesn't she, Corvus?" The crow smiled and sat beside the mirror. "Now on a more serious note, we are asking for your help again, but, first, let me explain why you are here. Not too long ago, you collapsed at a friend's house. And whenever a bad accident happens to you well, you faint. You know, just sit on that rock close to me and pay attention to what I say and see," said Right Whisper.

Janine made herself comfortable and waited patiently.

"Look right at me, Janine, and don't take your eyes off of me. Okay?"

"Okay. Will it hurt my eyes?"

"No. I promise. The bright lights will come on fast and then you will feel dizzy. That's when you will see yourself in your real life. Like watching a movie. Okay?"

"Okay."

"Ready?"

"Ready." Without warning, the magic began. Psychedelic wave of lights appeared floating in the air. "Ohhhh…would you look at that. What beautiful colors." She felt lightheaded. Then *Whoosh!* She was watching herself up close at her parents' friend's place.

"Would you like to see the ponies?" asked the middle aged woman. "I know you love horses. If you want, we can see them."

"Would I. Yeah!"

"I don't," commented Janine's younger sister, Elisabeth. "I'll stay inside and play with my doll."

"Speak better English, Elisabeth. It is not, 'don't' or 'I'll.' It is, 'do not' or 'I will,'" said Janine. "The English teacher will punish you if you speak slang."

"Other kids do it. So I will," snorted Elisabeth.

"I will have to agree with Janine. The English textbooks come from England and students from Canada are taught from those textbooks. But if you feel comfortable, Elisabeth, to speak slang, just do not use in class," said the middle-aged woman. Elisabeth nodded.

"I will follow the textbook," commented Janine.

6

"Stubborn," remarked her sister in frustration.

"Okay, then. That's fine. Elisabeth, you can turn on the T.V. if you want." The woman turned around to face the door of the house. "Get your boots on and let's go and see Sam and Jay." Janine was so excited to see the animals that she almost forgot to put her boots on as she headed toward the door.

"Boots."

Placing her left hand over her eyes, not concentrating on her real life image, Janine asked the crusty bark mirror, "So why am I here? It looks perfectly normal for me to feed and groom the animals outside the barn. I do not see any danger?"

"Keep watching Janine, for I am not finished yet," insisted Right Whisper, then *Whoosh* again.

Janine did what she was told. The world moved in the mirror until they were standing in an open field. It was clear that it was near the supper hour. Fenced in with a highway nearby, she was asked to lead Sam, to the barn, while the woman did the same with her other pony. As they almost entered the barn, Sam pulled back on the lead as he tossed his head up.

"Whoa!" Janine cried out.

"Hold him steady with your lead, and he will follow you."

"I am trying."

"Keep your distance from his hoofs!"

"He is up on his hinds!" she screamed as she clung to the lead.

"Hold on tight. I'm coming!"

"Hurry up, the lead is hurting my hand!"

The pony pulled away from Janine as the lead slipped from her hurting fingers.

While holding tightly on to Jay, the woman grabbed Sam's lead. "Whoa Sam. Whoa!" Almost instantly, the pony stood still and trotted to its owner as if nothing had happened. "There, everything is all right. He should be fine now. He was spooked about something. Ponies are like that."

Somewhat shaken and resistant in taking the lead, Janine said in a tremulous voice, "I do not know if I want to take him."

"Oh, stop it and take it. He's fine now."

"Are you sure? No, I do not want to."

"Janine, just take the lead. Jay needs my attention right now."

The pony seemed to have settled down. "Okay."

Her fingers slid over the lead and she stared up at the pony hesitantly as she pulled slightly. The pony lashed out, his teeth closing on Janine's back, who fell immediately onto the ground in a faint.

"Oh, no! Janine, Janine! Sam, whoa!" The woman quickly grabbed the loose lead and put both animals in their stable. She ran back to Janine and shook her gently as she tried to revive Janine. Glancing around, she lifted the still girl into her arms and carried her toward the house.

All of a sudden the bright lights turned off from the mirror, the scene disappeared and Janine sat still without saying a word. Her heart pounded, and she wondered what had happened to her after they got back to the house.

"Phew! We're back, Janine. And here you are." Right Whisper cleared her throat. "Are you okay? Janine, the show's over. Corvus, grab the velvet pouch by that rock over there and give it to Janine. Her panic and fear attack came back. She will need her magic walnuts for the journey to help her calm down. Janine! Snap out of it!" yelled the mirror.

Corvus followed her instructions. Within a few seconds, Janine had her walnuts in her possession. Ate a few, and she placed the pouch in her back pocket.

"I had no idea Sam would do this to me. He is such a good boy. Why would he nip me in the back like that?" Janine shook her head in confusion.

"Well, I am not sure about that, but you can count on the woman to explain it to you when you return to your real life," answered Right Whisper. "Now we must act upon your mission and complete the task at hand."

"Yes, yes of course. I will do my best to help you," assured Janine. "But... will I see my family again afterwards? Will I need stitches?"

8

"Eventually, you will see your parents and sister, but first, you must help us. I don't know if you will need stitches. I did not look at the gruesome stuff. I am sure you will be fine. And since you are with us again, that's a good thing. Isn't it?"

"I guess so."

"You don't sound sure of yourself. We really need your help, Janine," Corvus said.

"I do. I do want to help, but I am always afraid that things will go wrong, and I will not see my Maman, Papa and Elisabeth again," Janine said with a frown.

"Tell me; what are you carrying that rawhide bag around your waist for?" the crusty bark mirror asked.

"Oh! Yes! Well, Corvus found this pouch for me to carry you in while we... wait a minute. I do not really know where we are going," Janine raised her arms in the air.

"Interesting. Now listen carefully. We are to come in contact with a turtle named Tina. I do not really know when or how it will come about," Right Whisper said softly. "All I know is that Tina wanted to meet with you and has asked me to wait here until she arrives."

"Who is Tina?" asked Janine.

"Tina is a snapper and a friend of mine, but mind your manners. She can be a bit cantankerous."

"What does can..?" Janine stumbled over the word.

"Cantankerous. It means, having a bad temper at times, and it could be habit."

"Oh, I know someone who can be cantankerous at times. Not mentioning any names." Janine grinned at Corvus.

"Why are you looking at me?" asked Corvus defensively.

"Because sometimes you are."

"I am not!"

"Stop, both of you!" shouted Right Whisper. "Focus on the important matters."

"Sorry."

"Me too," said the crow.

"How do you know this creature will come today to see us?" Janine asked, bewildered by Right Whisper's request.

"Because you love anything to do with nature and its beauty, and this turtle may have a soft spot for a young girl's passion for it. With your upbringing from your immigrant parents, and proper manners and politeness towards mankind, you can be assured she will turn up to observe you."

"Will I be able to understand what she is saying? Or do I have to speak a different language? I only know three languages, French, German and pretty good English."

"Just be yourself, Janine. Don't worry about it. You'll be fine."

"What did she want to talk about? Did she say?" Janine kept slipping off the rock as she spoke so she shifted in an effort to balance herself.

"Not a word. She just instructed me that we be present here today."

"You know how shy I am. I may be too scared to speak to this creature, especially a snapper. I might run."

"Oh, don't worry. Don't be frightened. There is more to this mission than you think. That's why you will need your walnuts again."

"Of course there is!" Janine waved her hands in the air. Corvus shook his head and chuckled as he listened quietly.

"May I carry on?" asked Right Whisper. Janine motioned to continue. Her hands reached for her walnuts on their own accord and she felt a sense of calm wash over her. "All I know is that you will have to find out why there are acres and acres of lifeless trees still standing, but not decomposing."

"That sounds eerie. What am I to do with so little information? And who...Ooh!" She chewed a few walnuts without thinking.

"Exactly! Faeran, the phantom!"

Her heart started to pound, and her hands began to sweat. "Of course! Who else would do such a terrible thing?" She stood up to dry her hands on her track pants. "I don't know about this one, Right Whisper. I am scared thinking about it. I am only twelve years old." Janine began to pace and noticed black shadows appearing close to the forest nearby. The walnuts had calmed her down. She quickly walked towards the woods and shouted, "Go away! I am not afraid of you. I can see you behind those branches." Janine got closer. "Faeran, tell them to stay away from me! You do not scare me!" That was a lie, since her throat was dry and she was shaking, but it was the only way to make the shadows disappear.

"Ha, ha, ha! You don't scare us either," said a voice.

"I showed them. I feel better, now that I ate my walnuts. Oh! I did not see you behind me Corvus."

"Hm. Clueless sometimes. Just like the last time in the store."

"What did you say?"

"Nothing."

"I do not know where to begin. This is going to be a hard one. The shadows are here. I am not sure if…"

"Look, Tina will fill us in. You'll be fine. Corvus and I will be with you all the way." Janine placed both hands on her hips, and then walked away from her two friends.

"You must convince her, Corvus. Go talk with her, will you?" Right Whisper pleaded. Corvus flew off. He found Janine sitting on a rock as she gazed out across the lake.

"I know what you are thinking." Corvus proclaimed. "And I would be doing the same thing!"

"You do?" Janine stirred the water with her fingers as she sat on a flat rock. "You would?"

"I do and I would. But let's go beyond the worrying part and see if we can fix it," Corvus stated.

"Yes, but what if we cannot?"

"Then we, at least, tried, and you can go back to your real life with your family again. But I think, if all three of us like what we have done in the past…"

Janine interrupted. "You mean the three of us with our special powers that we carry or have in ourselves."

"Yes, exactly. What we can do to help with unfortunate situations. I mean, we work well together, do we not?" Janine nodded at the crow's question. "Well, then, why not try and see if we can find out why these trees are the way they are and solve the matter? You have always thought about solving mysterious situations in your heart, but never had the courage to do it in real life because of your age. So now is your chance. How about it, kiddo?" Corvus flew straight up into the air and immediately shot down like an arrow, just missing Janine by inches, and thumped on the ground several times.

"Ah!" shouted Janine, but then laughed at the crow when he did, too.

"Oh boy, that must have hurt. Give me strength." Right Whisper grimaced.

"Are you are alright?" Janine laughed. "I know I should not be laughing at anyone who may have hurt themselves, but you landed funny."

Corvus fluffed his feathers and checked himself to see if he was all there. "You never know what will happen…" He started to limp and winced. "Crap."

"Are you okay?" asked Janine, her laughter gone and replaced with concern for her friend.

"I just have to walk a bit. Ouch! I will be fine. Just give me a few minutes."

Janine placed both hands on her mouth to cover her smirk and turned around to look out at the lake as the water slapped the rocks gently. She thought about what Corvus had said of all the adventures and near-death experiences they'd had. That must mean something. Her friends needed her to help save or find out about what happened to the dead trees. "Sure," she nodded. "I will help you Corvus, but I…I already know what happened to the trees."

"You do?" he limped toward her.

"Of course I do. I do not think it was Faeran. I think that it was a forest fire. Caused by someone by accident or maybe even when lightning struck and started a fire. I am sure that is what happened," Janine triumphantly said.

"That is a good guess, but unfortunately, nope and nope. There would be split trees or char as evidence, but there was none."

"Are you sure?"

"Quite sure!"

12

"What about disease?"

"No signs of a blight or grubs have been found, I'm afraid," Corvus answered.

"Okay! Well, this sounds like a mystery to me. So you think that Faeran had something to do with this?"

"I am sure he was behind it. I just don't know how, why or what his motive was. But I am sure he is the guilty party. He's following you, isn't he? And when that happens, he's up to something."

"I guess those shadows I saw earlier were from Faeran's devious moves again. I hope you will be able to guide or protect me on this one, because if you are right about this…" Janine sighed. She stared out at the water again and wished that she was home with her family. "This journey will not be an easy one."

"I promise I will guide you and protect you, Janine. But remember, in the past we went through some difficult missions. This one will be no different. And besides, when have I ever failed you?"

Corvus flapped his wings to get Right Whisper's attention. Janine watched them from the corner of her eye as she thought about the journey. Taking a deep breath, she said,

"Okay, okay, I will help you, but you promise to be there for me?"

"Promise. Cross my heart." Using his right wing, he crossed his left chest. "Ouch!"

The two of them went back to where Right Whisper stayed, and made themselves comfortable beside her by the shore and waited for Tina. This gave Janine time to reminisce about her summer holidays with her family the year before and she fell asleep as she dreamed of her favorite camp ground.

A short time later, she woke up to Right Whisper calling to her.

"Janine, Janine! Wake up."

Janine sat up slowly and rubbed her eyes lazily. "What is up?" She yawned, so sleepy she forgot to cover her mouth. "Excuse me."

"You were yelling in your sleep," Right Whisper explained. "It sounded like you were in the middle of a tight spot. Is everything alright?"

"I think so. I was dreaming about last summer when some friends of ours chased my sister and me with rat snakes. I hate snakes."

"Mm, I love to eat them," Corvus said.

"Yuk," said Janine disgusted.

"Well, you were quite verbal while you were sleeping," said the crow.

"Was I? My sister says that I do this all the time when I sleep. Talk, talk, talk, talk talk…"

"It is never boring with you around. Don't get me wrong, I am not being smart, just observant. There is always something you have to chat about even when you are sleeping. I guess that is part of your make up."

"What is make-up?"

"Make-up?" the crow tilted his head at her as he gathered his thoughts. "It means, the part of your character behavior, like, you can be affectionate, playful, patient, **TALKATIVE**," Corvus said and went on to say, "whereas for me, well, I can be grumpy…"

"And cantankerous. That is for sure."

"May I continue?" Janine nodded. "Quarrelsome, sly, etcetera, etcetera. You get the picture?"

"How I was brought up, right?"

"Yeah. Something like that. Hey, you realize this is native country you are standing on and there is…"

"I know, this is Algonquin territory and an Indian reserve. Maybe Right Whisper's friend, Tina, will know."

"Oh, hello, Tina, I presume." Corvus said to someone behind her. Janine turned and saw a giant snapping turtle sitting beside Right Whisper.

"Ah!" cried Janine. It took her breath away, and she quickly moved away from the creature. Corvus shook his head.

"No," he whispered so Janine would remain where she stood.

"Ah, Tina, you made it. I was wondering when you would show up. Welcome!" said the mirror.

"*Aaniin ezhi-bimaadiziyan, niijii*? How are you, my friend?" the reptile said in a smooth voice.

14

"I am doing fine. Here are my friends that I mentioned to you earlier," proclaimed Right Whisper. "Come here, child. Don't be afraid."

"No." Janine shook her head. She felt frozen to the ground.

Corvus hopped over to Janine and his feathers brushed against her as he tried to move her forward. She said softly, "I had an idea you knew who was coming since you did not jump like I did? And besides, what did the turtle say to Right Whisper just then?"

"Well... I did in a way. And she spoke in Ojibwa saying, 'How are you, my friend?'" murmured Corvus.

"Oh! What do you mean, 'by in a way'?"

"I never really met her, but I was told that a friend of Right Whisper would join us and any friend of hers, is a friend of mine. I trust her."

"From J. Regia, the magic tree."

"Yup."

Janine glared at the crow. This was when she was annoyed with him. She snapped, "So why is it that you were not able to tell me in the first place? What other secrets have you not told me?"

"Well. There are times I try not to give you too much information, or else you may lose interest in our adventure."

"You!" Pointing her finger at him, she yelled, "I should trust you too!"

"You should. I am ordered to only say what is necessary. Only to protect you. The rest is my responsibility," Janine frowned at him. The crow tilted his head in sympathy, "I am sorry. I should have been more up front with you."

"I expect you to be more honest with me."

"I expect you to be more polite. I am sure that your parents do not say everything, just to protect you too."

"I do not know that but, perhaps?"

"Can I see you both, now?" Right Whisper asked noticing that Janine and the crow were in a heated discussion.

Corvus flew up and perched on a small cedar tree. Janine looked at the turtle and walked slowly toward it. It had a few short needles at the end of its hard shell, sharp claws and a long tail. She realized it was definitely a snapping turtle, and made sure to steer clear of its powerful jaws. She did not feel comfortable standing close to it and hoped Right Whisper wouldn't ask Tina to help.

"How do you do? My name is Tina. Don't be afraid. I won't hurt you," the turtle said in a shaky voice.

Janine crept towards the huge turtle. *Maybe she wasn't so bad.*

"Don't be shy. I won't bite." She smiled as Janine inched forward. "But you should know that if you cross me, well, I have been known to lose my temper once in awhile."

Janine stopped short. Her tummy did a little flip-flop. She definitely didn't want to upset the prehistoric reptile. She glanced over at Corvus, who was silent for once. She thought he must be analyzing the reptile carefully. She knew that if any danger came to her, he would protect her, no matter what the cost. But still...

"It is good to know how you operate, Tina. I will be watching you carefully, too," Corvus revealed as he gazed at the creature intently.

Tina tilted her head toward Corvus and acknowledged him with a slight nod.

"Fair enough. I may be of some assistance since I know the area quite well and the critters that live around here."

"Where did you get a name like Tina?" Janine asked, keeping well out of the turtle's reach.

"My real name is Cheldra Serpentine."

"Serpent is French for Snake, but Tina for short!" Janine interrupted.

"Smart girl." Tina gave Janine a crisp nod. "That is right. And rarely do we ever walk on land accept when we lay our eggs. Otherwise, we love to swim and walk underwater to eat weeds and scavenge for carrion."

"Carrion?" questioned Janine.

"Dead rotten flesh. We are scavengers just like crows." She looked at Corvus. "Isn't that right, Corvus? You feed on decayed animals?"

"Yuk! How can anyone do that? How can you eat such things? It makes me sick just thinking about it. Can you not just leave it alone?"

16

asked Janine. "It just turns my stomach whenever I hear that sort of thing."

"I understand. But when you grow older, you will figure out how the system of nature works, and why it is important to all of us," said Tina. Corvus watched the turtle move slowly towards the front of the mirror making sure she was of no threat.

Janine nodded in understanding. "As long as you will not do this in front of me or attack me, it is okay," Janine stated as she watched the turtle carefully. "By the way, do you speak native? I heard you speak a different language to Right Whisper."

"It is Ojibwa. It is the name of a tribe around here."

"Interesting." Janine looked intently at the turtle. "Maybe one day you can teach me. After all of this is over, of course."

"That would be my pleasure, Janine," answered Tina in a raspy voice.

"Well now, are we ready to continue with this journey or are there more questions for me to answer before I begin?"

Janine wanted to ask more questions about turtles and about Tina specifically, but knew they didn't have time.

"Where do we begin? How far do we have to travel?"

"Before I answer that, I need to tell you that you have very little time to complete your mission." The turtle moved slowly as she looked around the lake before she turned her ancient eyes back to Janine. "The trees cannot last any longer before they collapse and disintegrate."

"Wow! That sounds really awful. I do not know if I…" Janine's words trailed away and she walked over to Right Whisper where she stood by the rocks and water. Corvus followed and rested on a flat bed of grass about ten feet away from her.

"You will be fine and we will protect you," Right Whisper interjected. "But you need to know that Faeran our pestering phantom did this terrible thing to our trees. He did the same thing to the water. He claimed he needed to, to gain control for progress. What he has done to them, I do not know. A few chosen ones are still in the area, and are dominated by the phantom. The time will come when you will have a chance to change it back to its normalcy and he will oppose that threat. You can be sure of that."

Janine paced. "How will I ever stop this since Faeran has the power to do more damage with other small forests?"

"From what I understand," Tina said, "the phantom is looking for more souls, because he needs to have a hold over them so he can gain more energy and create more power within. We only have a few days until he inflicts more destruction. You need to move fast before that time. Who knows what he will do next?"

"How do you know?" Janine stopped pacing and stared at the turtle.

"Faeran loves a challenge. My sources keep me informed on his movements. Things will work for us as long as we outsmart him." Tina looked up at Corvus.

"You have your own spies?" Janine asked.

"Yes, but I cannot tell you who they are. Faeran has his own ears everywhere and if I say, it may put everyone at risk. We do not want Faeran to endanger those who help."

"That is why we have no time to lose," Right Whisper interjected.

"Correct! We cannot waste any more time with this matter. It must be done soon. But, before I leave, I must give you some directions and tell you who you are to meet before you begin your journey," Tina said.

"Are they your friends too, since it must be difficult to have…" Janine stared without completing her sentence.

"I have a few I can count on," Tina shut her eyes tightly and grimaced. "I need to go back into the water. You… you will meet Ci."

"Who is Ci?" Janine felt badly about the tears swelling up in the turtle's eyes.

"He is a Six Spotted Tiger Beetle." Tina panted. "Follow that pathway that runs beside Corvus. It won't be long before you spot a brilliant blue-green beetle, but beware its size. Faeran experimented with Ci and left him the way he is." Tina walked towards the edge of the water. "Follow his instructions carefully and he will direct you to the right path." She disappeared into the lake.

18

Chapter Two

The tree buds were blossoming and the different colors of bright, plush, greens; were vibrant. This was one of Janine's favorite seasons the end of spring when everything looked fresh and new. The fiddleheads from the ferns were plentiful. Wild strawberries covered the ground. *It sure would be a shame for all of this to be destroyed by Faeran, just because he wants to control the environment.*

Janine had convinced Corvus that it would be more convenient for the mirror to be transformed into a solid identity; as she had done during their previous journeys, than to carry ice in her pouch. Besides, the ice would melt and leave a mess. Corvus agreed and Janine carefully placed six inch by six inch Right Whisper iced face against a maple tree.

"I hope all will work out," said Janine as she took her time.

"Huh…here we go again. I hope it won't take too long like it did the last time," mumbled Corvus.

"She has had experience, Corvus. Give her a chance. Don't pay any attention to him, Janine. Continue," Right Whisper responded.

"Okay, here we go." Janine's right hand held the top edge of the ice and as her left hand held the bottom of it, so that the transformation would be a success. "I will hold your face firmly onto this deciduous tree since it is smooth. Are you ready Right Whisper? Because I am holding your face as steady as I can, and I am afraid I may let go."

"I am." Right Whisper pushed her face through the bark making a '*pop*' sound.

"It feels rubbery again. Let me know when it is safe to remove you from the tree."

Right Whisper made funny faces, by opening and closing her mouth and doing the same with her eyes.

"It is safe now."

Corvus knew what was going to happen next, so he covered his ears with his wings just to avoid hearing the mirror recite '*do, re, mi*' several times until it was all over. Janine grinned when she saw him.

Corvus led the way. Right Whisper was tucked into the old pouch around Janine's waist. She was impressed how the magical mirror was able to fit into her small pouch and realize that Right Whisper could suit up into anything. This meant her walnuts had to be placed into one of her track pants pockets for future use. Janine felt uneasy; afraid she would alert the phantom to their presence, and this was just the beginning of their journey. As they walked quietly, Janine vowed she would save the forest as best as she could.

It was not long before there was some rustling in the grass. She glanced down and searched the grass but was unable to find the source of the noise. Corvus was somewhat further away than usual and she could hardly see him. She hurried to catch up. Before she got close, several enormous dragonflies flew straight at her. She dodged them as best as she could afraid they would bite her.

"Corvus, where are you!" Janine screamed while she covered her head. "Corvus! Ahh, ahh! Come quick! I need your help!"

Corvus flew at the bugs, but there were too many and they were too fast for him to chase away.

20

"Get off me," she cried. "Go away! Where did these things come from? Help me Corvus!" As the dragonflies continued to hover over her, Janine dove off the trail and into the grass.

"Janine!" Right Whisper called. "No, don't run off the lane way!"

Janine peeked out from between several stalks of the tall grass lining the trail. The dragonflies abandoned their assault as suddenly as they had attacked and the swarm flew off as Corvus chased the few stragglers away. She crept out of the grass; puzzled. As she stood there watching them fly away, she felt something unusual on her feet. When she looked down, a black snake was slithering across her ankles. She realized she was surrounded by snakes of all shapes, colors and sizes.

"Ahhhh! Get me out of here! Ahhh! Corvus, help! Corvus!" She figured she was in the middle of a snake pit, because they were everywhere. Her heart pounded in full force.

Screaming, "How am I to get out of here! I can't move, Corvus! There is no place to go! Corvus, come quickly!" Sweat poured down her face. Her stomach lurched and bile burned the back of her throat. She could hear her heart pounding louder and louder. "I can't move. They are everywhere, and I feel sick, Corvus!" She started to cry.

Corvus flew over her, flapping his wings. "Listen to me carefully, Janine." He hovered over her and shouted. "As I move forward, you do the same." He fluttered his wings to scare the snakes away from her. "Janine. Listen to me." She blinked the tears from her blurry eyes and tried to concentrate on his words.

"Walk towards me," Corvus instructed.

She hesitated. "I am scared."

"I know, but you can do it."

She took one tentative step forward.

"That's it. Now another."

Janine followed Corvus's instructions, taking one step before she took another, her eyes focused on the crow. As soon as she was back on the main path, she crumpled and sat there sobbing uncontrollably. She never had such a shocking experience like this one before and she was scared. Not knowing the types of species these reptiles were, she was afraid they would bite her and become their meal. As Janine was still weeping and shaking, Corvus flew close to her until he landed and stood beside her, giving her comfort.

"You are going to be alright. Sit here for awhile and I will stay with you until you are ready to move on."

Still shaking, she nodded; grateful that it was over.

"You are safe now. Don't worry. We will continue when you are ready." The crow hopped around her as he looked her over. "I know I am repeating myself, but you are in shock and it is important you know you are safe now. I am so sorry that you had to go through such a horrid experience. Have some of your walnuts so that you will feel better soon."

"Where were you?" Janine shouted. "I called for help and you were nowhere to be found!" She reached into her pocket, grabbed a few walnuts and rammed a few of them into her mouth. "Don't try to pamper me with the walnuts stuff. I hate snakes. Give me time, but not now!"

"Janine, Janine!" Right Whisper interjected as Janine opened the pouch, still shaking.

"What!"

"Calm down. It is all over. You are safe now. They won't bother you anymore. They will not follow you."

"How do you know?"

"You are on the sacred path where you will be safe."

"I guess this path is not so sacred."

"I suppose. I tried to warn you beforehand about stepping away from the pathway, but you were too busy screaming and avoiding the dragonflies. They were to scare you and run you off the path. I, too, am sorry this happened, but don't be angry with Corvus."

"I wanted to come in from behind to get them off course and it would have worked, but too many others appeared from a different direction," Corvus remarked.

Janine stopped trembling and realized that she did feel better, especially after eating the walnuts. "I guess I was too scared. I wasn't thinking straight. I was so confused that I lost it."

"You will be alright, kiddo. You won't forget this for a long time, but you will be alright. I promise. By the way, you used slang words."

"I did?"

"I guess you were too scared that you weren't thinking, and it's okay. You don't have to be formal with us."

"Okay, then."

"What's up!" The trio jumped at the unexpected greeting, and turned to find a large, six-spotted tiger beetle approaching. "What's all the commotion about?" He bellowed. "Is there something I missed?"

Janine's eyes went wide at the five foot tall insect. Then she fainted. She went back to the dream she was in previously before Right Whisper woke her up.

****

"Ah, I just love this place. A three room cabin right by tall trees. We can spend two weeks camping," Janine said in a soft voice while she helped her Maman make the beds.

"Did you brush your teeth? If not, you must go and collect water from the lake and use that bucket by the wash basin," her mother would instruct in French. "We are low for the moment so we need more water for washing. Off you go with your sister."

"Hurry up Elisabeth! I want to go out and play."

"I'm coming!" she said.

"I cannot wait to find out what we will be eating here for the next two weeks. All I can think of is, the corn roast and hot dogs last year. Yummy. It is the only time we ever get it."

"Mmmm, I know. Let's hope it is the same this year," Elisabeth licked her lips, obviously thinking of the food.

"Let's hurry so we can play with our friends who I know brought their ponies, Sam and Jay. Maybe I can ride them."

"Oh no. Maman and Papa will not let you," said Elisabeth.

"Well I want to!" barked Janine.

23

"I will tell."

"My foot. I don't care. I want to ride them."

"Oh, oh, you swore."

"So?"

"You keep telling me not to."

"Come, let's get this done."

The girls finally filled the bucket of water from the lake when all of a sudden two young boys tapped the girls' shoulders from behind.

"Ahhh!" shouted Janine and her sister. "Get those things out of here!"

The boys swung black rat snakes by their tails over the girl's heads; laughing at them. Both girls ran so fast that they dropped the bucket of water. Janine could hear herself screaming.

"What?" the insect asked. "Was it something I said?" the insect looked perplexed.

"Janine!" Right Whisper screeched. "Janine, wake up!"

"Stay away from her," Corvus warned. He flew towards the lake and took a mouth full of water. He sprinkled it on Janine's face in hopes that it would wake her up, but she didn't move. Her eyelids fluttered and it was clear that she was dreaming.

"Try it again." Right Whisper urged.

This time, when Corvus poured water on her, Janine moaned but her eyes remained closed. After another attempt, she woke up, somewhat dizzy, but coherent.

"Are you okay?" Corvus asked.

She struggled to get up. "What happened?"

"You were screaming in your dream." Corvus tilted his head. "How do you feel?"

"Okay, I guess." She checked her arms and legs, just to be sure.

"Did I intrude in the middle of something?" the beetle asked, fluttering his wings.

"Do you mind?" Corvus focused on the insect's movements. "Janine met with some unwanted guests not too long ago, and she is in need of time to recover, so…so, bug off!"

Suddenly, without notice, two small chipmunks chasing one another ran right past them.

"You stole something of mine and I want it back," one of them said.

"You trespassed onto my territory first. So there!" argued the other as it avoided being caught.

"One of the locals!" said the beetle. "My name is Ci. I believe you were expecting me." He ruffled his wings again. "I will show you a place where she can rest. Right this way." Ci turned and walked down the path.

"Where are we going?" asked Janine.

"To my place," the beetle said without stopping. "Oh, by the way, I did not have a chance to introduce myself properly earlier since …never mind. My name is…"

"*We know; your name is CI!*" they all interjected from a distance.

"Oh! Surely! How can anyone forget? It must have been Tina who informed you. I never get a chance to present my name, or did I, and then explain how my name came to be. Someone always beats me to it. Why can't I get it out first?" He turned around continued down the pathway.

Corvus mumbled under his breath. "I think he is absent minded. That is what I think and *we* have to rely on this insect? This is going to be a long journey."

"What did you say?" Ci asked. He stopped and watched as the gang finally sauntered towards him.

"Get on with it Ci." Corvus turned towards Janine and smiled. "The sooner we are safe, the better we will feel." He turned back to Ci. "We are on a tight schedule."

"Alright, alright! Hold your horses. Now, what was I saying?"

"A safe place to stay." Corvus shook his head. "Oh boy."

Janine checked to make sure Right Whisper was securely tucked into her deerskin pouch and followed behind Corvus. Once again, they were confronted by the same two chipmunks running the opposite direction. They were still chasing one another and arguing over the same issue.

"Well, I want it back."

"You can't have it. So there," everyone had to stop again to give room for them to scurry by.

"Just remain on the trail and everything will be fine. Enjoy the view. On your left, you will notice different kinds of foliage and wild flowers while you are entering into the woods. On the right, the beautiful lake is quite picturesque with the sun shining on the water." Ci spoke as he walked and Janine found herself enjoying the beetle's constant chatter. "You will also see other trails to take, but beware. Some may not be so enjoyable, so make sure you follow my instructions explicitly. You do not want to make a wrong turn. I know how inquisitive you are, Janine, and it is okay to observe and learn, but sometimes if you take the wrong turn..."

"What do you mean, if I take the wrong turn?" Janine questioned. "Does that mean here or do you mean whenever I make the wrong decisions?"

"If you do not follow instructions, you may get you into trouble around here. We all make mistakes, but it is important that we also learn from those mistakes and make the best of it so that we can be at peace with ourselves." Ci bobbed his head. "Salamanders."

Janine frowned. "Pardon?"

"You will be faced with mean and fiery salamanders. They generally stay in their own turf, so you don't have to worry if you stay with me," said the insect.

"What do these salamanders look like? I don't think I have ever seen one before." Her stomach clenched and she glanced over her shoulder as she searched the edges of the path for these creatures.

"They are like miniature lizards of a sort."

"I don't mind lizards at all." Her tummy relaxed and she let out a sigh. "Why are they so dangerous?"

"Generally, they are not a threat. Actually, they are quite shy and stay buried under wet leaves or hide under debris." He looked at Janine reassuringly.

"What does debris mean?" she asked.

"Dead stuff! Well, out here it is called debris. Dead leaves that rot, fallen trees and twigs etcetera, and etcetera."

"Oh, now I get it. It is like what we put in the ground at home."

"What do you mean put in the ground?"

"Oh, like when my parents drink coffee and then throw the coffee grounds into our vegetable garden to help make things grow. It's called compost. Something like that?"

"I suppose so. You were not throwing out garbage, I hope?"

"No! We would never do that. Our fruit and vegetable garden loves compost. That's why we have so many healthy crops to eat. We have so much of it that my parents decided to sell them door to door or by the roadside. We sold lots."

"Well, now you know how important debris is to all of us." Ci stretched his wings out wide.

The crow titled his head and walked closer to the large insect. "Ci," Corvus said. "Tell me why these salamanders are harmful?"

Ci cleared his throat. "Ahem. Um, these particular reptiles are spotted salamanders and are about a foot long." He turned around and grinned at least, Janine thought it was a grin.

"Continue. You haven't finished your explanation, have you?"

"I haven't? Oooh! Where was I? Oh yes, I remember. These spotted amphibians generally spend most of their time buried under the forest ground eating earth worms, bugs…"

"Ci!" Corvus said in a loud voice.

"What?"

"Move on man. What happened to these reptiles? You got stuck on bugs!" the crow insisted.

"Mmm? Yes bugs. These yellow spotted salamanders were placed under the phantom's spell. He gave them flaming breath. He chose them because they can live more than thirty years. That is a long time to gain control and authority to rule the land." Ci gazed over their heads. "Faeran has that ability to change the salamanders and breathe fire, and we must change that."

"What are you looking at?" Corvus stared in the same direction as the beetle.

"Uh? Oh nothing. Nothing at tall."

"We will make sure to follow your lead," Janine assured him. They were getting nowhere with the way the beetle kept getting distracted. "Why are you the size you are now? Is it because of Faeran?"

"Who made her so smart? Who ratted on me? I want to know of your accomplice." Ci retorted.

"Is that why you joke or pretend to forget all the time? To cover up your pain? Is that the answer to your mistakes?" asked Janine softly.

"Alright, you got me. Well, almost got me." Ci stopped and turned around to face the group. "Kidding around helps me forget about my size. And it's a way of coping with what I have become. Now, what was the second question?"

"Being forgetful?" Janine reminded him.

"Yes! Faeran did his dastardly deed to me and once he realized that I was not going to be a threat to him anymore, he left me alone from that point on. I was no threat to him so he left me like this. Being forgetful. His dastardly deed."

"You already said that." Corvus rolled his eyes at Janine. She hid her smile at the crow's impatience with the beetle.

"So I did. So I did. I had hoped that he would change his mind, but he didn't. In fact, he kind of liked the way I had become and there were times I thought that he took pleasure in my new existence and being scatterbrained."

"Well, I think that Faeran thinks he can do whatever he pleases with others. He needs to be aware that not everyone is going to agree with his methods or changes. That is why we…" Janine pointed out when Ci interrupted.

"That is why you are here. Yes, yes, I know! Ah, now what was I doing? Ah, yes, now I remember." Ci turned, the conversation they had all but forgotten as he continued down the pathway.

Corvus shook his head. "Boy, are we in trouble," he muttered and let out a big sigh.

"I am sorry. Ci, but please believe me…us, we really appreciate your help in what you are doing. And I like your funny side," Janine remarked happily. Ci smiled at her and they continued on with their journey into the woods. Not too long after that, they came to a huge hollow tree with an attached basin about four feet from the base.

"Here we are," Ci said. "Home sweet home." He fluttered a wing at the tree. "Janine, you and Corvus rest in the burrow next to the tree. I'll keep watch. You never know how far Faeran may be. For all I know, he may be here now."

"Now?" she asked, her voice trembling.

"Don't worry, I'll protect you."

"Me too," cawed the crow.

"Now, what was I supposed to do?"

"*Protect this place.*" They all said. Ci nodded.

Janine, Right Whisper and Corvus snuggled into the burrow where they rested for a couple of hours. Janine was exhausted and fell asleep right away. After an hour had passed, Corvus, who never slept, grew restless staying in one place, grew restless as he waited. He turned to the large insect, his eyes flashing with impatience.

"Look, I'm going to inspect the territory before we head off together. You make sure to take care of Janine while I'm gone."

The bug bobbed his head in agreement before he guided the crow to the direction they were going to take. "Do be careful of Faeran. I have a feeling he is not far."

The crow took his advice seriously. "I won't be long. Keep an eye on Janine, will you? I trust you are capable of doing just that." Ci nodded and watched the crow fly away.

When Janine woke up, she felt much better than before. Ci was guarding his home like a trouper and was not aware that Janine was watching him. She slowly crawled out of the burrow, brushed off the loose dirt and debris from her body, and advanced towards the large bug.

"Where is Corvus?" she asked.

"Ahhh! You're awake!" the beetle fluttered his wings as he shouted in surprise. "I was not prepared for your presence so soon. I thought you were still sleeping. Although, I am glad you are alert and seem well rested. Are you?"

"Am I what?" questioned Janine.

"Rested. Is there an echo here? I keep hearing the same words."

"No, I don't think so. I was just playing with you." Janine smirked.

"Hmm, Corvus will be back shortly and I will stand guard until he returns, as promised. He is scouring the blue sky checking for any possible problems we may encounter. You can rest assured that he will have some news soon," announced Ci confidently.

"I think I will go back and sit and wait for Corvus. I'll rest some more. Thanks for the information," said Janine as she returned to the burrow.

"Good idea, great idea. I will continue with my duties," the bug informed Janine as she settled. He hesitated a few seconds before he asked.

"Janine? Hmm? What were my duties again?"

"Guard this area and me until Corvus comes back. Maybe?" Janine sarcastically answered with a smile. She watched as Ci stood there for a few seconds without responding.

"Yes, of course! Wow! How clever you are. Now why did I not think of that?" said the insect as he walked back to his original duty.

"Right Whisper, are you awake? I forgot all about you while I slept," Janine raised her eyebrow and tilted her head to the side as she took Right Whisper out of her pouch. "I hope I was not rude."

"Not at all." The mirror yawned. "I was glad to rest myself. That was quite the ordeal we faced earlier and I was afraid you would lose me in the field. It was a rest well deserved," Right Whisper affirmed intently. "How come you are smirking and shaking your head? Did I say something funny?"

"No, not you. Him. That Ci fellow. He sometimes doesn't make sense but it is funny to hear. Even though we have a serious trip to take, he makes it comical. I kind of like him. He acts like he cares, but in a funny way." She paused. "By the way, how do you know Tina? Why is she so important to our mission?" Janine made herself comfortable as she sat in the hideaway down by the large burrow and watched the insect muttering over and over of his duties as he safeguarded his tree.

"She's the one who knows who we can trust in this neck of the woods. Ci was her choice, and he will lead us to others who will help us restore the damaged forest," responded Right Whisper.

"I don't know about that. He doesn't seem to remember too much. I hope you are right. Or maybe you are not telling me the whole story. I feel there is more to it than just that," Janine complained.

"Tina is quite knowledgeable about the forest, and with what we have in store for us to solve, she is the perfect individual to contact. She would be very proud having us carry on her work on land, since a turtle of her kind generally lives near water," explained Right Whisper.

"I see. And what about those snakes? I was really scared when they crawled all over me. What kind were they anyway? I hope I will never have to go through that again for the rest of my life." She shuddered just thinking about it.

A shadow blotted out the sunlight for a second and Janine looked up in time to see Corvus landing. "The long black snake is called; a rat snake. It grows to about six feet long. It is the largest snake around here and it is non-venomous, so it will not take your life. The others, were garter snakes. These common snakes are quick on land and in water, and it's possible that there were young babies close by, too." The crow perched on top of Ci's hollow tree and watched as the bug walked around the tree, murmuring and totally ignoring the fact that the crow had returned.

"Would they bite me if you didn't help me walk carefully through them?' Janine licked her dry lips. "I was glad you were there, Corvus, because I didn't know what to do. It was not fun to watch a black rat snake crawl over my feet. I was scared."

"It is quite likely they were there on purpose since those big dragonflies nudged you towards that direction. It could be Faeran's operation to look for your weakness, and since it is late spring and all, snakes look for...Umm. Well, during the springtime animals or reptiles get together to umm..."

"Oh stop it Corvus." Right Whisper chastised. "You are not explaining yourself very well." She looked at Janine. "What he means

Janine is that, around this time of year, the snakes look for other snakes that are ready to become mommies and daddies so that they could have babies. That was probably when you came in the patch and found yourself in the breeding area. You were lucky that there were no little hatchlings, just adults. And yes, then they would bite if threatened." Right Whisper gazed at Corvus with a sparkle in her eyes.

"Am I ever glad I wasn't bitten by them or else our journey would be finished and I would not be able to go on."

"Guess you're off the hook," Corvus said to Ci, startling the bug. He turned to Janine. "It should be safe now, Janine. But before we go, I want to show you something special that is on a dock not too far from here. Then we will continue. I have already checked it and it is safe to walk down that trail." Corvus pointed out the pathway with his right wing.

Janine followed him. "That is strange that you would want me to see something when we have to get going with our tight plan." She quickly placed the mirror in her pouch.

Corvus remained silent until they reached the dock. "Have a seat," he told Janine.

"You want me to sit right here on the dock? But why? Nothing is happening," she said.

"Look." Corvus directed Janine to look at a dried post at the end of the dock. She squinted and tried to see what he was pointing at. Before long, she spotted a weird, ugly looking, sandy to grey, colored insect resembling a fat spider attached to a dried post. It had six legs instead of eight.

"What is that? It is *ugly*," Janine asked as she watched this insect make itself comfortable on a dried post attached to the dock. She positioned Right Whisper next to her to watch this odd bug. "Why is it staying on the one spot and not afraid of us?"

"Be patient and watch. It is one of the few times anyone is able to witness this next step and what it is about to do," Right Whisper answered merrily.

Janine did what she was told while Corvus also sat beside her with Ci just behind them. It had long slender legs, big eyes with a heavy body and small spikes sticking out of its back and sides. Everyone remained still for a good while, until the unexpected happened. Janine couldn't believe what she saw. Corvus was right. It was special. The ugly looking insect shuddered before it split open and a beautiful jade dragonfly emerged from it.

"What just happened here? I cannot believe what just happened. It is so unbelievable that it is magnificent," Janine said excitedly.

"Metamorphosis! That is what you have just seen. Is it not amazing how it all changed?" Corvus declared as he glanced at Right Whisper and Janine, then looked up and saw Ci.

"Wow! How does that work?" Janine watched the wet young dragonfly come out of the base of the ugly insect's head first and then the rest of the body curled itself out of the bug's body.

"Well, first of all, the name of the insect that you saw in the beginning is called, dragonfly larva," Right Whisper explained. "And you know that you breathe through your nose or mouth. Well, they have gills at the end of you know where," Right Whisper emphasized. "And when they swim, they squirt water out of their backside with such force, that you can see the spray on the water."

"Yuck! That sounds disgusting!" Janine declared as she watched the young dragonfly spread out its' wet wings to let the bright sun dry them. "And then what happens?"

"Then once matured after eating small prey, they will find a spot on either concrete blocks or stumps above the water that are dry, or even what you saw Janine, posts from the dock that it can climb to for its last existence as a young larva to give the dragonfly a chance to reproduce itself in dry atmosphere," Right Whisper continued to add.

"It is called a Rusty Snaketail…" Corvus added. "It's pretty rare around these parts of the northern forest."

"There's that word again. *Snake!*" Janine uttered with disgust in her voice.

"Look at their gleaming green eyes. Aren't they spectacular? Look up close and notice that their emerald eyes are widely separated, rather than touching one another in the middle of their head. They have a lovely mint green abdominal too. I detected that you were amazed at how it was spreading its wings and letting them dry out in the sun. Did you see the detailed tiny brown dots at the end of each wing and how shiny they were?"

"I think I will name it 'Rusty'. It has a rusty color around the stomach," said Janine. "Hi, little one!" She wanted to move closer to the dragonfly, but the crow held her back with one of his wings.

"Don't get too close, or else it will try to fly without drying its wings properly and die," Right Whisper said. "If the wings cling together, they will be useless to the dragonfly."

"Oh, then I will leave it alone. I hope that he will not be big like the ones who scared me the last time."

The mirror raised her eyebrows and said, "I don't know the answer to that one."

"I still want to call it Rusty and I hope one day it will be a strong flying dragonfly. I will leave you alone, beautiful little one."

Corvus signaled that it was time to leave. Janine nodded and waved at the dragonfly. "Bye for now Rusty. Hope to see you soon." She placed the mirror in her pouch.

Chapter Three

The weather was co-operating with clear blue skies and a bit of a breeze. The temperature was not too hot and everything looked so fresh and new. The snow had melted in the woods close by. Animals were waking from their hibernation. The buds from trees and shrubs had begun to sprout due to longer sunshine hours.

Spring was Janine's favorite season. She loved when the new greens came to life and the colorful, spring wildflowers bloomed. It was a busy time of the year. She hoped Faeran wouldn't destroy it all. They had to succeed in finding a way to revive the damaged forest so that the wildlife could carry on their normal life without being terrorized by the phantom.

They had just started walking again when the hairs on the back of her neck prickled. It felt like something was watching them. Corvus, who had been flying ahead to make sure they were staying on course, swooped down and landed beside her.

"Be careful," he warned. "There are some unusual shadows that appear to be watching us."

Janine looked back at the young dragonfly and was happy that she was given the opportunity to be present during its transformation. Her eyes scanned the water beyond the dock and she saw a head that looked like the size of a small fist sticking out of the water. Was Tina watching them? All she heard was an unusual breathing sound coming from that direction and, fifteen seconds later, the head disappeared into the water.

"Where are we going, Ci? This looks like a new pathway. I hope it is not a dangerous one like the last time."

"Come on, Janine. You have wasted enough time. Let's go!" cawed the crow as he flew in the air and fluttered his wings.

Janine walked closer to Ci, and glanced over her shoulder several times, but she couldn't see into the shadows. Before long, a short, painful screeching reverberation echoed through the woods. Janine jumped and huddled closer to Ci. She was sure it came from the dock, but she could be wrong.

"What was that?" she asked.

"I'm not sure," Corvus admitted. "Keep on moving Ci! We haven't got time to check out what just took place."

"But it came from the dock, Corvus!" Janine exclaimed. "I am worried that something bad happened to Rusty!"

"Don't think about it now. You must center your attention on the operation of getting to our destination. This may be a trick to delay us from our journey. Keep going!" Corvus insisted.

"But…"

"No *buts*! Go!" Corvus shouted and his voice brooked no argument. "I have to protect you from being captured by Faeran or his helpers, like the large dragonflies. You are in danger, Janine."

Reluctantly, Janine respected Corvus's orders and proceeded on. She felt sick to her stomach knowing something terrible had just happened and she was not able to check it out or even help. Deep down, she knew Corvus was right but that did not stop how ill she felt about the whole thing. As they carried on, Janine had to work hard in keeping up with Ci, since he had such long legs.

"Wait up, Ci. You are moving too fast. I know we are being followed, but I don't have the long legs like you do, you know?" Janine yelled trying not to trip along the way.

Ci slowed down a little. "Okay, but that rustling in the grass is our enemies closing in on us."

"Can you see who they are?" she asked, doubling over for a few seconds as her stomach twisted in pain and nausea.

"No! But I bet Corvus can!"

"Corvus!" shouted Janine. "Get us to a safe place! Anytime will do!" She hoped he had heard her for their safety.

"Come this way. Quick, Janine! They found us!" Ci bellowed as he changed course without warning. They were no longer on the pathway, but proceeded to take a different trail in the woods. Janine did not know if that was the right decision Ci made, nor did she know if he knew where to go. All of a sudden, the crow was flying right over their heads.

"Keep moving and don't stop!" the crow insisted. "These are dangerous salamanders that Ci mentioned before! Are you headed to that old red maple tree up ahead?"

"Yup! And we had better hurry up too! These little critters can run pretty fast and soon we will be barbequed if we don't reach the maple," answered the insect. "Janine, try to eat a walnut or two because these salamanders can smell your fear a mile away."

Janine followed orders, but fumbled several times until she managed to eat a couple. It was then she spotted a reptile that looked grotesque as it emerged from the ground and flung out its long tongue with a ball of fire.

"Yikes! Corvus, it's following me! Ouch! It just burnt the back of my hand! You little bugger! I am tired of this nonsense!" Janine jumped from side to side to elude their fiery tongues. "Ha ha, try to get me now!" Then she lost her footing and fell on the ground. As she looked around she noticed from the corner of her eye a dead branch and quickly picked it up.

"Take that and that!" She struck violently at the angry lizard, onto the grass, not stopping a beat. "Corvus help!" with her adrenaline rushing, her breath came in short gasps, she managed to take hold of her footing.

"Ooops! Corvus, my branch just caught fire! Ahh!" She instantly dropped the burning branch. "Now scram! Get lost!" Her muscles began to tense as a salamander slowly crawled toward her. "Corvus! I am in trouble here!"

"Look out!" cried Ci, as he, too, was evading the reptiles.

"I am trying to. Oh gosh, there is another one and they are lashing out at me! Corvus!" One of the salamanders lashed around her burned hand and pulled her off her feet.

"Ahhh! Ow, that hurts!" She crawled backwards trying to escape. Then abruptly she stopped and smiled at them. The salamanders looked perplexed.

As quick as a flash, Corvus flew in from behind and stabbed the ones that were close to her with his beak. All at once, they burnt to death. "Get up and run! More will be arriving any minute once they see the ball of fire. Run as fast as you can!" he hollered as he flew in the air. As more amphibians swarmed in, Corvus dove down and struck the salamanders numerous times to save Janine.

They continued on until the insect stopped in front of an old deciduous tree. From there, he hurriedly climbed it and disappeared into a large wooden bowl that was attached to the tree. "Janine," he called. "Quick, follow me!" Janine followed suit and stepped into the bowl herself, then slid down the hollow basin. She heard a click like a latch of a door from the top of the basin, seconds before she was plunged into darkness.

It was dark and dingy, and Janine was frightened. "Where are you, Ci?" She brushed off her clothes while her heart pumped quickly.

"I'm right here. Track my voice. Soon you will see a glow and then you will catch a glimpse of the illuminated roots."

"I don't see any…Oh my gosh! Yes I do. Is that ever creepy! Are those roots from underground trees that are lit? There are so many of them. I am amazed how bright it is down here. I cannot get over it and my eyes are going to have to get used to it, too." She rubbed her eyes.

"Yes, they are, and they will light up whatever route we choose to take. When we decide, they will turn off ten feet from where we left off," Ci replied. "And on top of that, if we need to reach a certain area in these tunnels, the roots will only glow if we stand near them until we don't need them anymore."

"So, now what do we do? I saw balls of fire come out of the salamander's tongues. That was scary! Will they not try to burn down this old tree or follow us? There were so many of them. And where is Corvus? Will he find us here?"

Looking at one of the passages in the tunnel, Ci answered, "I'm not sure he will, and no, they can't. It is a magic tree. You noticed that I was able to fit as I jumped into the basin?"

"Yeah. I wondered about that? Wow, that was amazing."

"Well, one size fits all. It will accommodate your size once you go through it."

"Swell!"

"But I was sure that I saw more of these creatures following us and probably trying very hard to burn it down." Janine caressed her injured hand. "Ow! My hand hurts a lot. Is there anything I can put on it to make the pain go away?"

"That is why we are not going out the way we came in. They are too dangerous," Ci explained. "They have tried it before but failed. They get electrocuted as soon as they touch the bark. It can sense evilness. Come on. I know where there is some cool water that will help your hand. It's not far from here."

"Oh, good. It hurts! Is it all because of the lights down here they get electrocuted?"

"Maybe. Or is it for a different reason?" the insect questioned himself but he gave no answer in reply.

"What about Corvus?" Janine said. "Where will we meet him?"

"Follow me. We must not waste anymore time," remarked Ci, as he headed down one of the root lined tunnels. "We'll have to go the long route through the shaft."

"Okay." Janine pulled out Right Whisper.

"Put her back!" Ci shouted. *"It will destroy her from all of those bright lights!"*

"Is that true, Right Whisper?" whispered Janine.

"Not that I know of." Right Whisper tried to say something more before Ci interjected.

"Now! Can we go now, Janine? I think we wasted enough time," Ci coolly said. Janine paused and stared at him. His attitude had changed from being funny to serious.

"Are we close to the water?" Janine tipped her head to one side.

"Do you ever stop talking?" He sighed. "We are almost there. As you can see, it is a long tunnel, but built up from the roots of the trees above. Mind the boulders and small stones along the way. This passageway will give us a chance to escape without Faeran on our heels. Hopefully, Corvus will find us before the phantom's force does."

"This place scares me." Janine followed along behind Ci. She glanced along the passageway and hoped they were safe.

Chapter Four

Corvus crouched high up in the magic tree and stared down at the ground below. Faeran paced in the small clearing near the tree as he listened to the salamanders' leader explain his failure.

"Sorry, your Excellency. We almost had her. My strategy was to surround the premise as close as we could, then isolate her from her friends and capture her without harm, as you instructed us to do. But she ran quicker than we'd expected her to. Did you know of her agility? Is there something we have not been told, your Excellency?" His muscles began to stiffen, and he tensed as his voice shook uncontrollably. "One of my soldiers even tried to scare her with his fiery tongue, but again, she escaped. You can be sure it won't happen again." He blinked rapidly and looked around for a quick escape from Faeran. The amphibian's body stiffened even more as he continued. "Your Excellency, we won't fail this time. Promise. But we were unaware of her dexterity."

Nodding his head, Faeran the phantom said, "It may have slipped my mind. I forgot to mention that she takes gymnastics and dance twice a week, but you are right! I should have told you. You did almost catch her; I'll have to give you that, but…" The phantom tilted his head and glided a little closer to the amphibian. "You see, your strategy did not work. You did fail!" retorted Faeran. "And for that, you will pay a heavy price."

"No, no, your Excellency. Give me another chance. I will not fail."

"Goodbye." The phantom's eyes burned into the salamander without warning. The amphibian screamed seconds before he turned to ash. "But she will turn up soon. You can be sure of that." He laughed loudly. "Let's go, guys!" He disappeared.

"Hmm, so full of himself that he missed the obvious. That's not like him. I wonder why. This was too easy. He never looked up," Corvus murmured.

Well hidden in the tree leaves, Corvus waited until all of the salamanders, except for one little one, had left. He cackled at this good fortune and dove straight to the amphibian, snatching it up and flying into the large basin of the magical tree. The salamander struggled to free himself from the crow's strong talons, and to keep from being electrocuted, but he could not escape. Corvus nearly lost his grip, but managed to hold on as he hopped through the tree's door. As he entered the corridor inside the tree, he spoke softly to the salamander. "Don't move." He knew that sound traveled and he certainly did not want Janine to be concerned or hear what was going on. He dug his sharp talons into his target. "Where was Faeran going? And why was he in such a happy mood?"

"You are hurting me. And I'm not telling. Go suck an egg, old bird," spoke the arrogant, young amphibian, flaring his nostrils.

"A young whipper snapper, are you? Are you sure you won't change your mind?" He dug deeper into his prey's tender skin until it began to bleed.

"I…would…be…careful if I were you…I may burn you up in an instant, old bird," said the amphibian. His breathing was shallower.

The crow did not hesitate to pierce further into the reptile's chest, feeling the blood oozing out as it dripped slowly onto his talons.

42

"Alright, alright. Cool your jets. Just ease the pain, will ya? You won't get anywhere if you continue. I will tell you what I know. Everything. Just lose the attitude and stop hurting me!" screamed the young amphibian, but was muffled by one of Corvus's wing to keep the noise down.

"Well, start talking. I don't have much time."

"If I tell you and the phantom finds out, you know what will happen to me. I will vanish into thin air."

"But if you do not tell me now, you will not see your friends ever again. I promise you that."

"Okay, okay, I get the drift. Your sharp claws are not helping here with my breathing." The salamander gasped to prove that he couldn't breathe. "I certainly don't have much of a choice, do I?"

"Nope. You don't. And I'll keep on pressuring you until I am satisfied. Get it?"

"Alright, alright then, you win. The phantom is happy because...can you let go of me a bit so that I can breathe and speak clearly? Geez, thanks. Because, he is expecting the second plan to work since the first one didn't turn out well just now."

"What plan?" Corvus asked, with a scowl, he released some of his grip.

"The plan was to capture the little girl. I think her name was Janice, Jane. Something like that."

"Janine, maybe?"

"That's it. Janine and...um..." The salamander was squirming a bit. "Well, you see. Can I get a little more breathing here? Thanks, not much, but thanks."

"I don't plan on letting you go."

"Okay, you're the boss. Don't look at me like that." The salamander squirmed and gasped again. "What I was going to say was our own leader decided to surround the area where Janine was headed, but that large bug had a better plan, and beat us all to that magical tree with the little girl, so we missed the chance of seizing her. The phantom was already prepared if the first idea did not work. He always has other plans if one doesn't succeed. He hates to lose.

And you can be sure there are consequences to pay. You saw what he did to our own leader."

"So what is his next plot?"

"His idea is to have his accomplice turn in Janine at a rendezvous close by the native reservation."

"Where exactly is the rendezvous?" Corvus insisted, but kept his voice down.

"I don't know! Before you get in a huff, I really don't know. We only follow him and the orders from our leader. But it did not pan out very well. That is all! I swear," spoke the terrified salamander.

"You mentioned an accomplice. Who is it?"

"I don't know that either," replied the amphibian without hesitation. Corvus narrowed his eyes but the amphibian was shaking with fright. It was clear he was being truthful.

"You don't have too much information about this capturing or else you are playing dumb on me." Corvus tightened his grip.

"Please, I really don't know. Believe me. Lay off, old bird. All I heard is that this accomplice is a bit forgetful, but can be counted on. The phantom has a hold on anyone he gets his hands on. If you know what I mean. Aaah, Aaah, you're hurting me."

"If that were true, how come your leader failed and the bug led a different way?"

"You are loving this, aren't you? How the heck should I know? I'm no mind reader. I take it you already know who the accomplice is." The salamander shrugged. "All I know is that Faeran let our leader have first try at the little girl, and if that didn't work, well then Faeran was ready for the second plan. That is all I know. I swear. Now can you let me go?"

Corvus loosened his grip. "Not a word to anyone about this or I will not be so generous the next time. I will let you go, but you must promise me that you will not obey the phantom's wishes. You must live your own life and be with your own class." Leaning back, Corvus stared at the amphibian with ease. "Off you go and don't look back."

"Don't you worry, you won't know I was here, I mean he won't know I spoke to you, nor will I tell anyone else," replied the amphibian as he dragged his injured body away from the crow.

Without touching the basin of the tree, Corvus shoved the wounded salamander out the magic door. He spun wildly through the air until he landed in a bush under the tree. For a short while, the little salamander was dazed and sore and didn't move. He then looked around to make sure no one was watching him, but he was wrong.

"Oh, it's you. I'm not a dope you know. I'm on my way. The right way. Aaah, it's going to take a while. See ya, old bird." Somewhat embarrassed, he slithered away. Corvus was glad he did not have to finish this young amphibian's life if he'd made the wrong decision. Hopefully, other salamanders would follow the same way as this little one did in the future and live happily the way they should.

Returning to the inside of the tree, the crow knew there was no time to lose. He had to be alert while he flew cautiously in the deep open shaft where he first heard the sounds. He did not want to be discovered just yet by the others, not until Janine needed him to save her from Faeran's assistant.

He flew as silently as he could and kept watch over Janine and Ci.

Chapter Five

"**W**here are we going, Ci?" Janine asked as she diligently followed. "Are those salamanders going to follow us?"

"Nope! They will try to burn down this old tree, but they will not succeed."

"Oh! How come?"

"A spell has been cast upon it preventing this tree from being destroyed," The giant insect trudged on.

"Who did it?"

"Who did what?"

"Who cast the spell on this tree?" She tilted her head to the side, building a slow smile. "You also said it senses evil."

"How the heck should I know? I just heard about a tale a long time ago, that this tree was magic." He shook his head. "I can't remember who said it. Anyway, can we cut the questions and keep…"

"What about Faeran?" Janine interrupted, while she examined her burnt hand. "Ouch! He will surely find a way to destroy it. Are we close to the water?"

"I'm afraid, in this case, he will not. Yes, we are close to the water."

"Oh! Why is that?" Janine asked with a note of surprise.

Ci continued to speed down the tunnel as if he was on a tramway.

"Because, there has been a rumor that he cast a spell on a Native warrior who also had powers to guard this beautiful forest, but the warrior only had time to protect this old tree from the phantom. Now, no more questions."

"Oh! I thought you said you could not remember who cast the spell on this old tree?" She squinted at the bug but a large smile filled her face.

"My word! Did I?" the bug wondered.

Janine's smile faded. She couldn't help but notice the change in Ci. He had gone from being forgetful to being agitated by her questions. She decided to push on and quiz him some more.

"What Native warrior? How come I never heard of this before?" Janine was thrilled to hear about a guard of the forest and hoped one day, she'd meet him.

"It is just a tale I heard as a youngster. A bit of a mystery because really, no one had ever seen this Native warrior before, or how he protected this old tree from Faeran. Now, what was I about to do?" Ci stopped and looked at Janine for a moment.

Janine pulled the mirror out of her pouch. "Did you know about this, Right Whisper? Oh, I almost dropped you. My burnt hand still stings." She tried to steady the mirror on her palm while she kept her distance from the insect.

"I was not aware of this particular tree and what happened to it through the powers of this guard."

"Did you notice the change in Ci's attitude?"

"I sure did. I wonder what triggered it. Shh, here he comes. Put me back quickly."

"I will try. Ooh, I almost dropped you again."

Ci glared at them. "Put her back," he insisted and walked on.

47

"What is his problem?" she whispered to Right Whisper. "Why is he so worried about keeping you in my pouch all of a sudden? Are you a threat? Or are you being protected for some reason?"

"I am not sure what his motive is. I can tell you that he is acting mighty strange since we entered the tree and that makes me feel uneasy and nervous. The lights do not affect my force. If you have the chance to place me down when he is not looking, you hide yourself so that you have an occasion to run the opposite way. Then we will know if he is trustworthy by his reaction," the mirror whispered back.

"I think you are right, but I will not drop you somewhere. We are sticking together. I don't want to be left alone in this tunnel all by myself. I do not know my way around here and I need you to be with me. Corvus is not here to guide me. It is too scary."

"Are you coming?" cried Ci.

"Coming." She stuffed the mirror half way into her pouch and walked slowly toward the insect.

Grimacing, and using her facial expression to pull herself into comfortable in the pouch, Right Whisper whispered, "Yes, I understand, but if we are separated, then Ci will have to look for one of us, instead of the both of us together. The way he is speeding us up, he seems to not have the time to look for us if we split up." Then Right Whisper raised her eyebrows, blinking quickly with her lips slightly apart. "Am I hearing voices not too far from here?"

"I don't hear anything."

"Quick. We have no time to lose. The sound is getting closer. It sounds like Faeran calling Ci. We have just a few minutes before Ci reaches them and I am not sure if we can trust him or not. I am not prepared to find that out and neither are you, Janine."

"I hear Faeran now. It sure sounds like a trap to me. But where will we go?"

"I am not sure what he is up to. And yet, Tina trusts him. Hmm, this is what is puzzling me."

"Now, that is a great feeling, is it not?" Ci seemed relieved after he heard what Right Whisper had just said. "Now put her all the way into your pouch." Janine hesitated but she did what she was told.

"Ohhh, yes Ci. It is a great feeling. You have been most gracious," Janine assured the insect, so not to sound concerned or confused with his latest comment. "But, before we go on, is there a place I can rest for a few minutes? My hand hurts, and we have not seen any water yet. We have been moving pretty quickly. And my asthma is acting up again you see and when that happens, well then I'm in trouble, so I have to take it easy and rest so that it will go away," Janine pleaded.

"Well, I suppose. The water is not too far," Ci answered reluctantly.

"How far?"

"Not far. But first we should reach the reservation, and then you will see some water. Trust me. Please, please, please," he muttered repeatedly under his breath.

"You promised me some water, Ci. Did you say the reservation?"

"I did."

"Oh boy. I have always wanted to visit the reservation."

"Great. I need to get you there safely first. Can you wait until then for your injured hand?"

"You bet I can. You just said it would only be a few minutes before we reach the reservation. The Native reservation? Did you not?" Janine declared and stopped to take a breath. She waited until the insect noticed her action.

"Yes... Follow me and I will show you where you can rest for a few minutes." Ci took her to a small alcove to rest and remained close as he paced.

After glancing at Ci to make sure he wasn't watching, she pulled Right Whisper out of her pouch.

"Now is the time to make a quick getaway," Right Whisper said. "You have no choice but to run when he is not looking. This whole thing is a trap. Ci seems too agitated when you asked for a rest."

"I felt that, too. If I rest for a few minutes, my heart rate will slow down and my asthma will be under control. But I really want to head for the Native reservation."

"I realize that, but I am hearing strange sounds not too far from here, and I think it is Faeran," the mirror answered.

49

"Oh? I thought Ci was Tina's friend."

"So did I. I guess things change, people change, but who knows? He may have changed his mind to help us." Right Whisper sighed.

"Which way do I go? This is a strange place and the roots glow wherever I move along. I am lost here and I am too scared to move without him. Who knows what he might do if I run away from him? He may bite. Have you seen those chompers?"

"I understand. Have a few walnuts before you go and then think about running a race. Do it when you are ready. Don't go until his back is to you, though, and then run like the wind."

"Okay. I will have a few walnuts now and I will make my move when I am finished." She popped a couple of nuts into her mouth.

"Are you ready to go?" Ci peaked around the corner of the alcove. It spooked Janine a little. "And what did I say about Right Whisper? Put her away."

"Okay, okay. I am putting her away." She finished off the last little bit of the nut in her mouth and waited for the right time to take Right Whisper's advice and scurry in the opposite direction.

"Place me back into your pouch snug as a bug and don't look back until you feel you are safe. Got it?" Right Whisper whispered. Janine nodded. As soon as the insect was not looking her way, she darted.

Chapter Six

Corvus continued his trek down the passageway. He flew low to avoid the stalactites hanging from the ceiling. Occasionally, he had to dodge a boulder on the floor of the tunnel. Determined to find Janine and Right Whisper, he listened attentively for any sound that would tell him where they were. He couldn't let them be captured by Faeran.

Eventually, there was a dim light, off in the distance. Why are there no lights in his pathway? He pondered as he cautiously headed towards the illumination. It was not long before he realized it was Janine headed towards him.

"Quickly, Janine this way!" he cawed.

"Boy, am I glad to see you. Thank goodness you are here. I was worried. I was not sure which way to go, but I did not want to stop. Where are you going?" All of a sudden Corvus disappeared. "Where are you, Corvus?"

Ci's jaws bit down on Janine and he held her in mid-air. "Ahhhh!" screamed Janine.

The large insect instantly let go. "Phew! It's a good thing I found you. You ran the opposite way. You can get lost out here. Were you?" Ci articulated as he bent down and stared at her face.

"I...I...I was what?" Janine stammered.

"Lost, silly. Who were you talking to just a moment ago?" the bug inquired.

"I was talking to someone." She shrugged. "I cannot remember."

"I know the feeling." He sat on his hind and stared at nothing for a moment. "I would say something or do something and then forget where I was going with the conversation or what I was supposed to do. Anyway, you were going the wrong direction little girl. Let's go." He headed back the way they had come, glancing into each passage they passed. "I swore that I heard you talking to someone. It sounded like Corvus." He shrugged. "No matter, maybe I am hearing voices now. Hope it will not be another added problem I will have to deal with. Too many challenges for me to face right now. Oversized, forgetful and now I am hearing voices. What's next?" he muttered.

"Now what?" Janine whispered to the mirror.

"Corvus is near, do not fear too much. And stay alert," Right Whisper pointed out. "Maybe, he is on the level. We will have to trust him for now. We do not have a choice and I would not send you down a strange passage."

"I don't feel brave right now," Janine confessed, but followed the bug reluctantly and hoped he really would lead them to safety.

Chapter Seven

"They should have been here by now your Excellency!" remarked a frightened salamander. The other salamanders were anxiously shuffling back and forth as they waited with anticipation. They were anxious to find the little girl as planned, and their patience over doing nothing was wearing thin.

They would pick fights among themselves just to check out their sparring abilities as to how they can outsmart their opponent and to just pass the time away or choose a brave salamander to join their circle. Anything to break the monotony as they waited. Of course they knew that if they crossed the phantom by being too abrupt with each other, their lives would be at stake and may die if they were not ready to strike when ordered. It was about a half hour later when a brave salamander questioned Faeran about where they stood.

"Your Excellency, how much longer? We are getting impatient waiting for Janine to show up."

"*Quiet!*" Faeran raised his long thin arms. "I did call him. It won't be long now! He knows better than to cross me."

"Who... who... who's he?" the salamander stuttered.

"Ci. And if I were you, I would not risk your life right now when we are so close. I am not a patient kind, but the rewards are worth it. I get the soul and you get the girl. Don't spoil the fun." Faeran slowly turned and gazed into the amphibian's eyes. "And you, you little short stuff of a soul, you have a lot of guts. More than the last one that just got fried. So you have just been promoted. You have become their leader. But remember this. One wrong move or word and you're toast. Understand?" Faeran glared at the amphibian in front of him.

"Yes sir, thank you, sir. I will not disappoint you." He tilted his head from side to side.

"Now then, I hope that you all have your picks of the day and will concentrate on a bigger fish," said Faeran, facing the opening of the tunnel.

"Ha, ha, ha."

It was not difficult to hear the phantom's callous voice once Janine and the mirror came close the opening of the tunnel. Janine knew then that the bug played a trick on her and they were going to be in Faeran's hands soon. If only there was a way out. But where?

Her eyes scanned the tunnel for any way to escape but Ci turned around and grabbed her roughly again with his mouth and threw her into a small cave. Before she realized what was happening, the insect covered the entrance of the cave with boulders and a small avalanche filled in the rest of the gap.

"Help! Help!" she shouted. "Get me out of here! I can't see. It's too dark! Corvus!" Janine quickly sat down to catch her breath. "I cannot breathe, Right Whisper. I think my asthma is acting up again." Her shallow breathing and wheezing tightened her chest and she rubbed at the pain there. She knew that she had to concentrate on breathing slowly as best as she could and not speak in order to alleviate the pain.

"Take deep breaths and try not to panic. I am sure that Corvus is nearby. In the meantime, sit on the ground with your head down and breathe slowly."

Janine did what Right Whisper had instructed and focused on her breathing as her head hung between her knees. After a few minutes, she felt better and could breathe easier. She sat up and stared at wall of boulders.

When rescue didn't come, she sat back and looked around the cave. Burning torches hung on the cave walls, and she grabbed one and scrutinized the area. It helped her feel a little safer. The flooring was covered with rocks and pebbles and, the walls were made out of stone. While over her head, stalactites hung down from the ceiling. It may be granite, limestone or a marble mineral. She wasn't sure.

"Too bad I do not have time to examine these rocks. They look interesting to me. Maybe another time." It was hard to tell which mineral it was, since it was too dark to describe. Remembering that Right Whisper was with her, she took out the rawhide pouch and opened it wider.

"What do you suggest we do?" She pulled out the mirror and set it gently on a boulder. "I have no idea where we are or why we are here." She hugged herself and looked fearfully around. "Right Whisper? I'm scared."

"I can see that. I am puzzled myself, but I do believe we were placed in here for a purpose."

"Huh? We were not placed! How about thrown! I've got cuts and bruises to prove it."

"Nevertheless, Ci saved our lives and it is up to us to figure out what to do next before Faeran figures out what just happened. Let me think."

"Why didn't Ci say something before…before all this."

"Well, remember his condition. Maybe he had second thoughts. Tina picked him to help us in the first place. She was the one who said we were to trust Ci. So I guess I still have to believe that."

"I hope you are right." Janine wiped her face and ears with her jacket. "Yuk, his saliva doesn't smell so good either. And my hand still hurts. I hope we find water soon."

"Why don't you look around to see if you can find something that will get us out of here?"

"All right," Janine glanced around the cave where the light from the torch could reach. "This is such a small cave I doubt there is anything here but stones and sharp rocks." She put her palms on the ground to push herself up and yanked them back. "Ouch!" She looked at her hands particularly her burnt one. "See what I mean!" She brushed off her hands and looked around for some way to get herself free from this imprisonment. Her strategy was to start at one end and carefully move clockwise around the room until she could find a way out. It was not until she was half way around that she let out a scream. "Ah! Oh my goodness! Look Right Whisper. Look at what I just found!"

"Bones and a small skull. It is hard to tell how long it has been here. It looks like a child's body laid here. Poor thing."

"Does that mean we will be here for the rest of our lives? I mean, my life?"

"No, don't think like that. Think positive. Something happened here. I admit, but that doesn't mean it will happen to you. Keep going. There must be a sign or an indication as to how to get out of here. Keep looking."

"Ouch! Not again." She rubbed her cheek. "Another scrape on my face. I won't be able to recognize myself after this." It didn't take long for her to explore the entirety of the cave. She'd come up with nothing. Flopping down on the cold floor of the cave, she shook her head. "I guess this is it. There is no way out. It looks like the bones will have company in a few days."

"Don't talk like that! We will find a way out. Just sit tight."

"How long will these torches last until it will be total darkness?" She looked around the cave and shuddered. "It's cold." She adjusted her clothes and tried to stay warm.

"Janine, you are a life saver!"

"I am?" she asked, confused.

"Go around again, but this time look at your flame and see if you can find incoming air or a breeze."

"You know what? That is an interesting fact. How come we are not without air? We seem to be breathing quite normally and my asthma is not acting up right now."

Janine walked carefully around the perimeter of the cave and this time watched the flame instead of the walls as she looked for any unusual air currents. She was about to give up when the flame on her torch fluttered ever so slightly.

"I think I found it!" she squealed. "Look, Right Whisper."

"Good. Let's see if you are right. Try to move the boulder."

Janine leaned her torch against a boulder and studied the rock that blocked the breeze. She ran her hands over the stone and found a smooth part on the side. Placing her hands on it, she pushed slightly.

"Argh. Ouch! My hand hurts. It's no use."

"Use your body to balance yourself. It may work better for you, since your hand is aching."

"Okay, I'll try." She shifted her body against the boulder and pushed with her back to it.

It did not budge. She pushed again, harder, using the side of her body, her feet planted to the floor. She gave a little squeal of excitement as it shifted slightly. The flame on her torch flickered rapidly, and she knew there was more air on the other side of the boulder.

She held onto the edge of the boulder, but this time she pulled and before she realized what was happening, the boulder dislodged. It rolled across the cave floor and bounced against the opposite wall, brushing against her shoulder as it cleared past.

"Ouch. That hurt." She winced and rubbed her shoulder. She peered into the opening left by the boulder. She could hear water flowing. Grabbing her torch and Right Whisper, she inched her way into the hole and realized that she could stand up. Not much of a change from where she'd come from, except bigger rocks laid around her. She took a few cautious steps further into the cavern until she spotted a pool of water. Zipping up to it, she placed the mirror in her pouch and secured it into her jacket. She was prepared to hit the water when she heard Right Whisper screaming. She pulled the mirror out of her pouch.

"Right Whisper, what's wrong?" she asked before she continued. "This is some kind of a river. I guess I'll have to jump in and see if there's a way out. But first, I must place my burnt hand in the water. Ahh." She dunked her hand in the water several times and then used the ribbon from her hair and wrapped it loosely around her sore hand, not thinking of the black feather.

"What are you doing?" Right Whisper cried. "You have no idea what is in the water or out there!"

"We have no choice. Corvus can't save us in here. So I either starve to death or take a chance and swim to the other side. What will you have me do? Is this the end of my journey, Right Whisper?"

"No! Think positive. I thought that we could be free another way. Like another gap somewhere else or a different way out. I never thought there would be an underground river especially, from around here. I thought this was only a forest."

"What do you want me to do?"

"I guess, use your instincts and hope for the best. You are right. Corvus can't save us here."

Once the mirror was put back into Janine's jacket, after making sure the pouch was secured, Janine put her feet into the water.

"Brrr. It's cold." She shuddered, tied her hair into a ponytail without the ribbon and checked her aching hand.

Making sure again that Right Whisper was securely tucked away before going any further, she waded into the water. Gasping at the cold, she smiled when she realized that it only came up below her shoulders. That would mean that she would be able to walk through the water with light from her torch to give her guidance.

"Boy, am I glad I don't have to swim. I must not slip and fall right now. I must steady myself. These stones underneath are slippery. Ohh." She lost her footing. "That was close." She frowned as she balanced her body in the water.

The water was cold, but refreshing. The river was narrow, and she had to be very careful not to slip since the edges of the river were hard stone that were sharp and dangerous. That was easier said than done, for she did slip a couple of times adding more cuts and bruises on her body, but still held on to her torch.

"Ow. That hurt. I hope I can get through this." Tears flowed down her cheeks from the pain she had to endure. She wiped the tears from her face and walked carefully in the water analyzing every step she took.

She handled the torch like a pro and it was not long before she had to stop to catch her breath. She looked around her and observed that there was a wall that stopped her from going any further.

"Oh no! Now what? Well, I am not giving up. There must be another way out." Water was escaping from somewhere under the surface, so she inched along the wall until she found the spot. She would have to go underwater to see what was on the other side of the wall. She let go of the torch, held her breath and dove under the cold water. Kicking her legs with all her might, feared that her lungs would give out and she'd have to draw in a breath of water, made it to the other side of the wall without a problem. As she surfaced she caught a glimpse of light up ahead. The water was not deep and she was able to stand.

"This is better than I thought. Oops. The stones are still slippery." She had to hold onto the edge of the cave to catch her balance since there was a small under current beneath her. The cave was much wider now and she was able to swim freely towards the opening where she could see the light of day.

When she reached it, she came upon a small beach that had fish skeletons on shore. Janine wondered where they'd come from, since she had seen no fish in the water itself. She walked a few steps away from the dead fish and sat there for a second or two before pulling out the mirror.

"Are you okay Right Whisper? We seem to be safe now." At least, she didn't see anyone else.

Right Whisper coughed several times "I am fine." She sneezed, and Janine looked at her dubiously. "Truly, I am fine."

"Where are we?" Janine looked around again. "I wonder if Corvus will ever find us here."

"That is a good question. A good question indeed! Let us rest for awhile. I am sure you are tired by now."

"I sure am." She took off her jacket and laid it across a nearby bush to dry. "I think I'll hide in the bushes until I feel safe. And maybe I'll dry out, too."

Chapter Eight

"**W**hat!" Ci said as he reached the edge of the tunnel, fully exposing himself in front of Faeran and the salamanders. He gave an incredulous glare at their faces as they looked at him, perplexed. "What! Why are you all looking at me like that? Have you never seen an insect like me before? Come on, guys. Faeran?" The insect gasped as he stood still with his head tilted. He knew that the phantom would either destroy him instantly or demand an explanation as to why he'd appeared without Janine present. He was prepared for the worst.

With a hard glare at the insect, the phantom spoke in a low monotone. "Where is she? Where is the girl, Ci?" Not a sound was heard as they all looked at him.

He made a show of looking to see where Janine was.

"I swear, she was right behind me. Honest, Faeran. You have got to believe me!" In his mind, Ci went over the steps to make sure he did not miss a beat. He sat down at the edge of the tunnel. "I shall investigate and cover all of my moves," he said in a sheepish voice. "That's what I will do."

"A deal is a deal. You assured me, no you guaranteed me, that you would personally deliver Janine right to this door step and hand her to me. You failed me!" cried the phantom.

All of the amphibians let out a sigh. They'd seen what had happened to the salamander that had failed. Toast. Faeran was about to throw flames from his bony fingers and destroy the insect, but Ci disappeared behind the tunnel's wall.

The phantom's anger grew. "Eventually, you and I will meet. The only question is when will you give up. You will in the end. These creatures will accept what has just happened and as you know, they will not give up so easily under my command. I will destroy you. Now is a waiting game. You have to accept it. Face it, Ci, you can't wait forever!" The phantom's anger turned to laughter. "I have some other errands to attend to, but my compatriots here have but one mission to take care of and that is to wait until you show up and surrender. It may be a long, long time before you change your mind, but no worries; they have all the time in the world. Sooner or later, you are mine to do with as I please." Faeran faded away, his evil cackle trailing along behind him.

Ci was shaking, hiding behind the wall of the tunnel, he heard every word the phantom had to say. He needed time to think things through. If only he could remember where Janine had escaped to. Something happened back there, and he couldn't remember. He had such a hard time retaining information since Faeran's evil magic had absorbed his soul. The phantom had crippled his mind and body through his fear. He just couldn't remember. The phantom could not touch him at the moment, but he was right about one thing. He couldn't remain in the tunnel for the rest of his life. Pushing away his fear, Ci decided to retrace his steps to see if he could recall a little bit of what had happened to Janine. Slowly, observing every inch of the way, the lights in the tunnel lit up as he revisited his former passages. He looked high and low trying very hard to retrace his actions.

"Where the heck did Janine go? How long has it been since I saw her last? Let me see. I saw her when we were talking about water and going to the reservation. Then I asked her to follow me so she could rest, and I placed her in an alcove, I think. This is all giving me a headache. I must find her. I can't give up now."

He'd covered most of the tunnel when he heard a strange, faint noise. It sounded like a fluttering sound close to his direction, but he could not see anything. He stood still for a few seconds, listening, but picked up nothing and continued with his mission. After extensive investigation, he decided that his task was at an end when again he heard a weak sound. He thought it was coming from around the next corner. Sneaking over, he peered around the bend. Corvus was pecking at something on the floor of the cave.

"Ahhhh," Ci cried. "What are you doing here?"

"What a ridiculous question! What do you think I am doing here? Going on a holiday?" Corvus declared.

"Are you?"

"Certainly. I love checking out the root of a tree."

"You do?"

"No!"

"No?"

Corvus cawed angrily. "No! I am looking for Janine. And if I recollect, you were the last one to see her. So?"

"So, what?"

"So, where is she, Ci?" The crow approached the bug up; his eyes sparkling with anger as he drew close.

Concerned about what Corvus would do, Ci backed away from him.

"I…I seem to have lost her, somehow. You know, I thought I heard you earlier speaking to Janine. Was I right?"

"Maybe."

"Maybe? Well, whatever. Just before you came around the corner, I was retracing my steps."

"Explain."

"I made a bargain with Faeran," the beetle stopped as Corvus hopped angrily toward him again. "But really, it was a fib. I mean, he thought that I was going to deliver Janine to him since he cannot enter this magical tree and I can, so he placed me in charge of arranging to have her fall right into his hands. Only, I wasn't going to, really!"

"Where is she now, Ci?" Corvus stared at him, not quite believing the bug.

"That's my point. I looked everywhere. I can't remember where I saw her last."

Chapter Nine

Janine was restless and could not relax. She turned to the mirror, which she'd rested against a bush.

"You know, Right Whisper, we cannot stay here forever. We have to find our way out. Maybe then, Corvus will find us."

"I hope so," answered Right Whisper.

"Me, too! Are we to wait for him?"

"If you feel like remaining here, I will not argue with you, but if you want to leave, then it's okay with me, too. How is your hand, anyway?"

"It is still painful, but if I keep dipping it into the water, it feels better. If we have to leave in a hurry, I have no idea which way to go. I'm kind of scared Right Whisper, especially without Corvus here."

"I know what you mean. You can use your walnuts to help calm your nerves."

"That is a good thing." She pushed her hair out of her face. "I dare not call to Corvus, for fear the phantom would hear."

"That won't matter, since Faeran can detect your fear of the unknown. You know he feeds on your soul if you show fright of any kind. That is why Corvus can protect you. The phantom cannot sense the crow's fears, since he has none. Which is why Faeran despises Corvus."

"I wish I was like that. Then I would not have to worry about saving the trees."

"We need to carry on and, hopefully, meet up with Corvus."

"True! He may have some ideas as to which way to go since he can see up ahead. But first, I will just sit here by the bush beside you and dry for a little while longer." She fell asleep, and it was not long before she dreamt of the outcome of her journey.

****

Janine picked up the mirror and placed her securely into her pouch. She studied the area and tried to figure out where to go. It was a good thing that the weather was cooperating with the sun-shine giving her a chance to clearly see her surroundings. It gave her a peek at the kind of terrain she was up against. Her instincts told her to move forward, and she set off at a steady pace. There was a lot at stake. She stumbled through the terrain. Over rocks that littered the ground and through thick bushes that she had to push aside. There were times that she slipped and fell onto the sharp edges of the rocks scrapping her ankles and knees. Shortly after stumbling, she noticed in her dream, some blood dripping from her ankle.

She hobbled over to a small patch of moss and collected some to soothe the pain, placing the moss against her injured ankle. She looked to make sure the mirror was intact. She sighted a grassy hill up ahead and decided to climb it. Struggling, she finally reached the top. It seemed to take a long time to move her body to the top of the hill. A large rock blocked her view. So in slow motion, she shifted her body to the right to see what was on the other side. Then she heard her voice.

"Oh my!" she yelled. "Oh my goodness! I can't believe this!"

"Janine! Janine! Wake up! Janine, wake up!"

"Ahhh? What is going on? What happened?" Janine responded, totally confused.

"You were shouting 'Oh my goodness'," answered the mirror.

"I did? I thought I was awake. I was sure of that."

"Well, you were very much asleep. And so was I until you began to cry out."

"I guess I was dreaming. Thanks for waking me up."

"Do you know what you were dreaming about?"

"I am not sure. I thought I was wide awake and we were on our way up a grassy hill. When I got to the top, I looked over a huge rock. There were many natives with beautiful costumes and colorful feathers chanting and looking up at me. It was strange to see natives appear in a meadow filled with wild flowers, along with roaming dogs and happy children laughing, giggling, chasing one another between teepees." Janine wondered why they had all looked up at her. "What does that mean, Right Whisper? It was then that you woke me up."

She didn't wait for a reply. "Let's go Right Whisper. I need to check something out."

"What?"

"I want to see if I can find the same spot." She got dressed and tucked the mirror back into the pouch and set off.

"I hope I can remember where this place was. It looked so real." But she soon realized that the landscape in her dream was different. Maybe the grassy hill did not even exist.

"I was so sure there was a hill around here somewhere. I was so sure, Right Whisper." Tears welled behind her eyes as she removed the mirror from her pouch once again.

"Don't despair, Janine. Sometimes these images appear in the most peculiar places. Strange as it may seem, I think you are going up a hill right now," the mirror remarked.

"What do you mean that I am going up a hill?" Janine asked.

"Well, look at the horizon. It is not flat behind you. You have climbed up so slightly that you never noticed the rise," said Right Whisper.

Janine turned herself around and examined her footing on the ground. She realized there was a slight decline if she moved backwards. The mirror was right. She had climbed up a slight hill. They were at the top. Matted grass and jagged rocks littered the area, but no huge rock or natives were in sight.

"Oh darn. Right Whisper, I goofed. I thought there would be some clue on the other side of this hill, or a beautiful meadow. But all there is, is a dirt road with a half rundown shack across it. It looks so…"Janine's voice trailed off as she looked around her sadly.

"So upsetting. Is it not?" added the mirror.

Janine nodded. "What happened here?" She continued to gaze at the location. "I don't understand all this. Normally, my dreams don't let me down. There has to be an explanation for all of this."

"Probably, but changes do occur. You must come to terms with that in mind. What comes next will happen in due course, and it might be to your advantage. Right now, just be patient and maybe we will be able to receive answers from your dream one day."

"What do you mean by 'what comes next will happen in due course'?" Janine questioned.

The mirror did not answer right away, and she wondered if there was an answer.

"Well? What did you mean by that statement?"

"I can't explain it. Your life is like a history book and, in life, you move on creating your own history. Maybe you will come to understand as you move on with this expedition or, maybe, the answer will become clear later on in your life. It may make sense one day. Or maybe not ever."

"It was a great dream and it made me feel important," Janine responded.

"Shall we look below and check out this poor looking house and see who lives there?"

"It looks deserted. I hope it won't bury us when we check it out. Or maybe it is a trap. Who knows? Maybe Faeran is waiting for me."

"Tell you what. Why don't you leave me here on the hill. You can prop me up on that rock over there and if someone is coming, I will let you know."

68

"That sounds like a good idea."

"If no one is around, come back and get me. For I, too, want to look around in the shack. It looks interesting." Janine followed orders and after a few minutes of checking around and not getting an alert reaction from the mirror, she returned to the hill. Janine immediately tucked the mirror into her pouch and into her jacket. Removed her ribbon from her hand and re-wrapped it lightly again. She made her way toward the building, since she was as curious as the mirror, as to who lived there.

Chapter Ten

Sitting on the edge of his seat, the phantom was surrounded by followers in his chambers. His trusted security guards stood beside and behind him on an elevated, flat platform dressed in black robes and hoods, with knives tucked into the white sashes around their waists. Under the spell of the phantom, the security guards were young men who had become his slaves, were his feed for power. The other guards, who were on watch, were located at each entrance of the cave's chambers wearing outlandish black, long coats and hoods with spears in hand, were also under the command of Faeran.

"They are all mine," he chuckled. He gazed down at the floor, smiling as strange, lizard-like beings, grotesque in their stature, slithered by his feet; although they went nowhere. Other abominations slid up and down the walls or leapt gracefully from place to place but remained in the same area. Constantly in motion but never moving forward.

Far away from the cave where Janine had escaped, Faeran's chambers had a stone floor, ten feet wide by twelve feet long, adjacent to other small chambers. The tunnel was attached to an ancient cave belonging to The First Nations people. Sacred carvings on the walls represented indigenous spirits, images of plants and animals, shamans and reptiles. Having control of this particular tribe and their sacred forest was only the start of his mission. Destruction of their existence and souls would give him the power he craved. The only thing standing in his way was that brat, Janine.

He pushed away his irritation at the thought of the girl and instead, sat back on his throne and enjoyed every minute of his status. He'd wait until the right moment to seize her. He was confident that the little girl would appear soon, and it was up to him to thwart her task of saving the lifeless trees.

Corvus, on the other hand, was a different matter. Not being able to infiltrate into the bird's mind and soul would be a challenge. Faeran needed to divert the crow from his own mission of guarding the girl. He must use his wit and charm to help persuade the crow to follow a different route away from the girl. If he was away, he wouldn't be able to save Janine's soul. Examining a potential candidate carefully, he halted all of the crawling creatures near him.

"Stop at once, all of you. Do not move one inch. Stand where you are. I have a mission for one of you." He rose and strode toward the center of the well-lit assembly room. His two trusted security guards, who'd stood beside him, followed, ready for any command.

Taking his time, the phantom tapped his lips with his elongated index finger and meticulously studied each and every beast standing before him. His idea was to pick an elderly, disposable participant, where the mission had to be described with precise instruction, a genuine errand, to be able to convince the crow to assist him.

"I need a volunteer to help me find a crow named Corvus. Now who shall I pick?" He pointed at a slow moving, nineteen inch light grey amphibian with dark spots and a feathery external gill on its head. "Is it you?"

Next he pointed at one that was yellowish green with two rows of red spots outlined in black. It had a crooked long tail making it about five inches long. "Or you!" He glared at the two possible contenders

71

standing before him. "You!" The victim was immediately grabbed by the phantom's security guards.

The creature with the feathery external gill struggled, "Let me go!" The creature's eyes went wide. "The crow is considered the most intelligent bird and Corvus will not bow to you." The creature continued to struggle and nearly slipped free of the guards before they tightened their grip. "You are wasting your time. The crow is about rebirth, reflection and healing. He will know I am lying. He is magical. I will not lower my high regard toward the crow by having him assist in your wickedness you so portray to all of us." The creature managed to squirm free and tried to flee.

Faeran pointed at him. Fire shot out at the creature, catching him seconds before he slid out of the cave. Screams filled the air seconds before it burst into ashes. "Ah, what a shame. You just can't' get good help these days." He regarded the remaining creature. "Who wants to be next on the list? I hear there are advantages and disadvantages to this job. I always have to do it myself. Now, since the first choice was not as cooperative as I thought and dared to defy me." He glared at the other creatures before he turned to his guards.

"Ha, ha," he laughed as though he was sharing a joke with them before he carried on saying. "Cremation of all things was his choice. Can you imagine thinking that way? I suppose he wasn't that interested. Oh well." He pointed to the same amphibian he'd pointed to earlier. "...you are my next contestant. You are the lucky one." Faeran blurted out as he directly faced the elderly creature. The amphibian eyes met the phantom's and he knew his choice was minimal.

"Your Excellency. What is it you would have of me?" The creature's voice was smooth, he dipped low, his charm dripping as he tried to convince the phantom that he was a humble servant. It was necessary, regardless of what the command would be.

He pushed aside his past but it still bothered him. He had been a Native elder before Faeran had turned him into this grotesque creature. He knew the crow was an intelligent bird and, if he were to sway it to co-operate, he would have to be cleverer than it and the phantom, in order to free his soul. He bowed. "Tell me what you wish me to do."

The phantom examined the amphibian for a moment and liked what he heard.

"Perfect! Maybe too perfect." Faeran strode back to his throne, and then turned to look at the chosen one. The guards dragged the creature and dropped him in front of the phantom's seat.

"How nice of you to drop in without a fuss. It is so enjoyable to work with those who are so obliging. Now you, my little, friend, will have the privilege of becoming who you were before. A shaman or a witch doctor or something like that. I can never tell the difference. How does that strike you?"

The elderly amphibian nodded again. Faeran continued on, "as you may have gathered, Corvus is the protector of a little girl named Janine. I wish to grab her soul. You must provide a diversion that will lead Corvus to another path so he is not there to protect her. Once I have her soul, I can fully destroy the forest."

He sat back and tapped the arm of his throne as he assessed the amphibian closely. He waved his hand and the creature cowered at the gesture. "How you do it, I don't really care, as long as the crow in not in my way. I am well aware that he is quite smart and all that jazz, but you, as a priest of some sort to your people, can convince him. Tell him you need his help to save an injured party or some sort of casualty that needs his attention immediately. Can you do that for me?"

The amphibian nodded.

The phantom adjusted his cloak before casually incinerating another amphibian. The elder didn't wince as screams filled the chambers.

"I must warn you that the crow has great spirit within itself," the amphibian said hesitantly. "But I will do my best to speak the truth about an incident that will be of interest to him."

"As long as it does not interfere with my plans, old man. You don't want to waste my time. I don't take failure very well. As a matter of fact, I get quite agitated and furious if you disappoint me.

Get my drift?" The phantom was examining his lengthy nails. "You know of the casualties that will occur to your people. You would not like to have that upon your shoulders, would you?"

"No."

"Excellent! You have two days. I don't care how it is done, as long as it is done.

If you do not fulfill your task, you understand what will happen… You will… how shall I put it? Depart from this life, kick the bucket. I like that one, don't you?" He started to cackle in front of his congregation. "Do I make myself clear?"

"Perfectly," the amphibian answered.

Faeran's piercing orange eyes glared at the creature.

"Don't mock me, old man, for you are on borrowed time. Oh, did I say that out loud?" He touched the creature with his bony hand and laughed.

The amphibian transformed into an indigenous old man. "Don't disappoint me, old chief. I will be watching you until the girl is safely in hand."

"I will do my best to fulfill your wishes."

Chapter Eleven

Once again, back to his old self, the shaman could feel the same aches and pains that he'd lived with for what felt like an eternity. "Ow." He shook his head, but checked himself realizing that his long white hair and delicate body were still intact.

Everything was as it had been before the transformation into an amphibian. His body felt the same as he remembered. He was still wearing his old, deer tanned robe, shirt, breechcloth, leggings and moccasins. In addition, around his neck, he wore his favorite string of white and purple beads. His deer hide robe included porcupine-quills embroidered along the sides and front of his coat, and his leggings had the same faded embroidery at the bottom. He touched his leathery, well tanned skin from years of sun exposure, but his heart ached for his people whose freedom had been taken by Faeran during their Pow Wow ceremony. He had to make it up to them. He could not fail.

Sad eyes were all glaring at him, not a sound was heard from anyone; except from the phantom's parting words.

"Do not disappoint me, old chief. For I will be watching you until the girl is with me."

The old shaman nodded. After his people bid him farewell, he was escorted to a secret wooden door. One of the guards unlocked the door and shoved him through. He stumbled, '*Aah*' but remained upright with effort. He looked up at the sky. It was the first time in a long time that he'd seen daylight and he wanted to enjoy the warmth of the sun on his skin. But, after a few minutes, thoughts of finding Corvus and saving his people invaded his mind. He wondered how he could introduce himself to this crow without arousing his suspicion. It would be a challenge.

The shaman looked for a place to camp for the night, where he could build a fire and hope that Corvus would present himself. Would the crow believe his story? He didn't know.

His only refuge was to return to his old family dwelling hoping it was not occupied nor torn down since it was a shack with no running water or electricity. There was a clearing a short distance away that would provide enough shelter and he headed towards it, gathering some dead grass, a few twigs and a medium size branch to build a fire. After he got to the clearing and built a fire, he decided to rest and think about what he was going to say to the crow. After several hours, he made a decision. He would shape-shift.

Chapter Twelve

The crow folded his wings in front of him and repeated to himself, No, no, no. It's not true. To Ci, he asked. "Where are you taking me, Ci?" The crow watched the insect walking in circles.

"The last time I saw Janine was right about here. I swear. Then I...oh, what did I do next?" The bug sat heavily on the ground, shaking his head and muttering. "I am totally confused Corvus. I am afraid that I have failed you and that we will not be able to find Janine in time."

"What do you mean, not find her in time?"

"If she is missing, Faeran will find a way to locate her."

"How can that be? You told me this is a magic tree that he can't enter. The crow frowned and waved his wings. "Are you saying that she may not be here at all?"

"Possibly."

"Either she is here or she's not. Which is it, Ci?"

The big bug crinkled his forehead. "I got it!" He walked along slowly, looking closely at the tunnel walls.

"There should be a small cave around here. I pushed her in it. And then... I can't remember."

"Well, that's a start. You said around here, did you not?" questioned the crow.

"I think so. I am pretty sure, Corvus."

The two spent about twenty minutes walking slowly down the tunnels before Corvus became aware of what looked like a cave in. On closer inspection, he realized that it was several large boulders covering an entrance.

"Is this it, Ci?"

"It might be."

"Let's check it out since we have nothing else around here that looks odd."

Ci immediately removed some of the small stones and rocks until he uncovered a small cave beyond the boulders. Corvus would have no problem entering it, but Ci was too big, so he continued to move several large boulders. It took all of his strength to take it out which ultimately had him lose his balance. "Whoa." He went head over heels bouncing off the other side of the tunnel wall.

"Quit fooling around, you big goof. Get over here and help me!" cried Corvus from the other side of the entrance.

"I'm coming. I think I can squeeze in here. Oh my goodness I have to lose weight." Ci grunted as he pushed himself through the hole.

Corvus spied a torch burning close to the cave wall.

"Take that torch so we can see what is in here. It is very likely that Janine was placed here." They scrutinized the area.

"Well, not exactly."

"What do you mean, not exactly?" The crow approached the bug deliberately.

"Well, you see, it was like this. I had this brain wave to get rid of her instantly and pushed her into the cave so that the phantom would not harm her." The bug grimaced at the crow.

"She better not be hurt or you are mine. Do you understand?"

"Fully understand. Fully."

78

Moving on to inspect the area, Corvus noticed that one of the torches was missing from its sconce. He was certain Janine had passed by here. The flooring was covered with rocks and pebbles; the walls made out of stone and over his head were more pointy minerals, which he had not experienced before. The place was too dark to identify the different minerals glittering in the torchlight. They continued on.

Before long, they spotted an extracted boulder leaning against the side of the wall. They moved quickly towards a small hole. Ci had some trouble getting through again, but managed with a few scrapes and bruises, and they crawled toward the sound of a waterfall.

"Ow."

"Use the torches, since they will guide us and let us know which way the flow of the air is coming from," said Corvus. They walked carefully onto bigger rocks, toward the sound of water until the rocks came to an end and the water was in sight. They spotted a pool of water below with the same sharp rocks protruding from the top of the cave. Corvus also noticed a black feather lodged between two rocks. The only way to get out of the cavern was to swim into the water and see what was on the other side.

"Hmm." Corvus turned to Ci. "She was here. Are you up for a little swim? It could be dangerous and we have no idea what is out there or if there is something in the water."

"I guess you have a favor to ask me, don't you, old boy?" The bug put down the torch and headed towards the water ready to jump in.

The crow hesitated for a second or two. "I guess I do, but don't let it get into your head."

"We have no choice, do we? Shall we?"

The crow grabbed the torch with his beak and hopped onto the bug's back seconds before Ci jumped in. The water was not deep and Ci hurried along. "Ohhh." The water was just over his long, spindly legs and off they went dodging rocks and sharp edged ceilings. When they got to the place where the water poured through a hole in the cave wall, he hesitated. It was clear they were on the right track to locating Janine since a floating torch was visible. Corvus let go of his torch and clutched onto Ci.

"Well, what are you waiting for? Dive in already."

"I will as soon as you take your wings away from my eyes."

"Oh, sorry."

Ci frowned at Corvus, took a deep breath, and dove into the water.

"Ugh, ok…" Ci coughed, expelling fluids everywhere including on Corvus, in order to breathe from his lungs. Corvus, still clinging to the bugs back, wiped off the smelly fluids from his face. He caught a glimpse of light ahead and demanded the bug speed up his pace.

"Come on, let's hurry up." But the undertow was wicked and it swept them away, battering against the rocks. After several long minutes, Ci managed to right himself and crawled onto the sharp rocks that lined the river.

"Ouch." He looked to see if he could find Corvus. But he was nowhere to be seen. "Corvus. Where are you?"

Before Corvus knew what had happened, he was gasping for air. He tried desperately to answer Ci and stay afloat, but crows are not great swimmers, and he kept hitting sharp edges that knocked the breath out of him. He made numerous attempts to get back on his feet. Finally, he got a bit of luck and grabbed a rock with one of his wings and pulled his body as hard as he could, but failed. He tried again, but knew it was no use. The current was too strong.

"Ci, can you give me some help here?" he shouted. "I don't know how long I can hold on."

As Ci lay gasping for air, he spotted the crow lying limp by the edge of the wall. He made a mad dash into the water to retrieve the bird, but as he headed toward him, he discovered another problem. Something strange was coming toward him, fast. At first he could not make it out, but when it got closer, he knew they were in danger.

He didn't have much time. He needed to save the crow and then deal with the intruder. Ci moved Corvus out of the water onto a bed of small pebbles and then turned to face it. The only way to defeat his opponent was to face him head on. As he prepared himself, he realized that he was looking at a huge mottled sculpin, a type of fish. The tail and the dark blotches gave it away. It had razor-sharp teeth that could rip Ci apart. Faeran had bewitched it, creating a gentle fish into a flesh eating monster.

When it reached him, it jumped out of the water and latched onto Ci's cheek. "Ahhh!" His immediate instinct was to bite into its side. Generally a small fish, the large size gave Ci a chance to hold onto it better. They grappled in the water, splashing and biting and snapping. Ci squeezed the sculpin as hard as he could until it finally stopped thrashing. Blood was everywhere and Ci felt his body was broken from the battle. Pain almost overwhelmed him but he pushed himself toward Corvus and scrambled from the water. He was worried other sculpins would smell his blood and come to attack them. "We need to get out of here, fast."

He made his way back to the crow, who lay limp and unmoving. Ci nudged him. "Don't die on me now, old boy." Not getting a response, he quickly picked up the bird. Slipping into the water, he swam swiftly towards the bright light. He kept saying to himself, "I've got to get out of here." He looked back, and saw several fins swimming toward him. His adrenaline rose, and he swam as fast as he could, slipped once or twice, but caught himself. He finally made it to shore. Quickly, Ci spit the bird out of his slimy mouth.

He promptly jumped on the bird's chest in an effort to get water out of his lungs. It was then Ci realized that one of his legs was not functioning. It was badly mangled, but he would worry about that later. Right now, he needed to save the bird and get away from the water.

"Come on, Corvus. You can't give up on us now. Besides, you are supposed to be the strong one. Let me try this again." He started to pump the crow's chest again.

After the third time, he was ready to jump when he heard the crow cough, "Over my dead body. You try that again and I'll deck you. Ugh! Get your slimy, drooling saliva out of my face! Yuck."

"I was only trying to help. I realize jumping on you was a bit harsh, but someone had to do it. I had to do something to get you to breathe. A simple thank you would be appreciated, you know."

"Fine. Thank you. Yuck!" The crow wiped his face with his wings. "One word of this to anyone and I will personally make your life miserable. Now get OFF of my chest!"

"Oh. Yes. Sorry." He slowly removed his legs off the bird's chest and sat quietly. They rested on a tuft of green grass. Corvus watched as Ci licked his damaged leg.

The crow sat in front of Ci. Coughing, "That looks painful. Did you scrape yourself on one of the rocks?"

"No. It was one of those." Ci pointed at the channel of the water.

Just then a mottled sculpin lunged at Corvus from the edge of the shoreline. Ci pushed the crow aside and bit off the fish's head. The crow watched as Ci then ate it.

"What in tarnation was that?"

"That…" Ci crunched down on a bone, and then licked his legs, "is a mottled sculpin. Courtesy of our enemy, Faeran. Generally, they're smaller in size and only eat greedily on small females. Only this time, they…"

"They?"

"Yes. They were supposed to destroy us since there were no females that I saw in the water."

"How do you know there were no females?"

"The females literally fall head over tail toward the male because they are in love. Then the females turn topsy turvy to lay their eggs near the male's burrow. It is then…ouch!" screamed the bug who tried to straighten his injured leg without success. "I'm afraid, old chap, that this is the end of the road for me. My leg is immobile and it hurts terribly."

"No way. I am not leaving you here all alone. Besides, you saved my life twice and now it is my turn. Let me try to locate a splint and tie it somehow. I should not be long. I must find a nurse tree. Give me a few minutes." Ci nodded.

Corvus flew around a little, and soon returned with a long narrow branch, a hollow maple bark with some green moss on it, long, thin, white dead grass and cedar branches and laid them beside Ci.

"What are you planning on doing with all of that?" asked the bug.

"Well, first of all, I want you to prop yourself up and lean on something solid so that your battered leg is exposed to me. Here let me help you up." The crow gently held out one of his wings to help Ci up until he was able to hold his own balance against a boulder. "Then I will try to straighten your leg so that I can tie a splint to it. It will hurt like heck for a while, but it will mend on its own, and it will get better every day. The part you have to do is help me place the narrow branch against it, so that I can put the hollow maple bark around it and tie it with the dead grass."

"So what are the cedar branches for?"

"Ah! Good question. In case you should lose your balance and fall, it will soften the tumble and also mask the smell of dead flesh. The moss will help, too."

The bug just stared at the bird, "Okay."

"Go ahead! I've been through pain before when…" He watched as Corvus hopped around, tying his leg into the splint. Ci shrieked "Ahhh, watch it, old boy." He winced whenever the crow touched it. Whether the procedure was an accomplishment or not, the insect felt it was better than waiting for death. Ci did not want to die alone anyway. It was important to move on.

"There!" Corvus fastened the final tie securely around the moss and cedar branches "That should help you walk for a little while, but remember, you must rest so your leg will heal properly. And don't put any weight on it if you can."

"That will be difficult since all of this is new to me. But, I am glad you are with me Corvus."

The crow was surprise to hear the last comment Ci just made. Corvus grabbed one of the insect's uninjured limbs with his beak and looked at him for a moment. "I am here because of you and Tina, but my main goal is to protect Janine. I will do anything to keep her safe and, if I find out otherwise, old chap, your life is on the line. Are we quite clear?"

Having some difficulty due to the stabbing pain in his leg, the bug finally answered the crow.

"Quite."

"Good. I will look for a walking stick where I looked for the bark. Don't go away!" The bird flew away, and returned within minutes.

"Now you will rest for a short while and then I will scour up ahead to see if there are any signs of Janine. I will be gone for about a half hour. Afterward, I expect you to be ready to journey on without too much stress since you rested. See that boulder over there?" Ci nodded. "Lay against that rock covered with moss and grass." Corvus waited until the bug moved over to it. Ci chuckled. "Hmm." Then settled down against the rock with great difficulty since; he had never had to deal with a splint before. He then closed his eyes.

The crow knew the bug was in shock and he hesitated on leaving him. The distress the old beetle was going through could cause further injury. He watched Ci as he slipped into a light sleep before falling completely asleep. Corvus flew off to look for Janine or any sign of her. It was not long until his magical senses came into play. He found a spot in the grass that appeared to show where someone had sat down. But he saw no one. He started to fly back to get Ci, but felt drawn to investigate before he woke Ci. Jogging his memory a bit, he then remembered this had happened to him a long time ago when he was much younger.

Chapter Thirteen

Janine walked slowly down the dirt road towards the ramshackle building. When she looked at it, an overwhelming feeling of loneliness pressed against her, filling her with an almost debilitating sense of isolation. Overgrown bushes and scrub brush surrounded it. There were numerous ferns, countless seedlings from four hemlock trees that stood by the house and blood root plants. White daisies and yellow buttercups grew amongst the weeds.

Where was Corvus? She hoped he would find them soon, because, even though Right Whisper was with her, the crow would help her feel safer.

"What do you think, Right Whisper? Should I find out if anyone is living here?"

"That is up to you. Remember, we are looking for the exact passage to enlighten our way to the dead trees," answered the mirror.

"I know, I know, but somehow this place seems so peaceful and intriguing that I want to inspect it. Maybe, it will give us a clue as to how to get to there."

"I just hope Corvus will find us soon and that he is not in trouble, because we absolutely need him as an extra pair of eyes and protection." Right Whisper echoed her thoughts.

"Me, too!" There were quite a few wide open cracks on the rundown shack. The windows were boarded up. She stepped gingerly on the dilapidated porch and tried not to step on the broken glass as she peeked through the cracks between the boards that someone had nailed over windows, but it was too dark to see inside. "I wonder why these windows are covered the way they are?"

Glancing at an old rocking chair in the corner of the porch, Janine carefully opened the aluminum door. She waited for her eyes to adjust to the dark, and then stepped inside. Squinting, she looked around. A tiny ray of sunshine filtered through the space between a few of the boards. But before she went any further into her investigation, she let out a holler alerting anyone who might be in the house.

"Hello? Is anybody here?" She took a few steps further inside. "Anybody here?"

Being inside the strange house reminded her of what her Maman told her when she was younger. She'd climbed over the backyard fence in the wintertime, to see what was on the other side. Of course her Maman thought her daughter was well secured in the garden, but little Janine went to investigate outside her home. She had wandered into a stranger's house and ended up watching a black and white television in her snowsuit. Boy, did she catch it when Maman found her. Now, inside another stranger's, house, she felt guilty, but she just couldn't keep from being so inquisitive. She had to know why this old home interested her so.

"Well, Right Whisper. What do you think? Should I go on?"

"Do your best not to touch anything, Janine. It is invading someone else's privacy. Or it could be a trap. Just be careful," commented the mirror.

"That is a hard one. You know I cannot promise you that, but I will try," she teased.

She gazed through the dim light at the tired room that was in need of great care. The sun rays shone through spider webs that took over every nook and cranny. The dust was about an inch thick. A tired brown couch sat in the corner. Across from it was a fireplace. Adjoining the living room was the kitchen, which came equipped with a sink and stove. There was a spigot for water down a narrow hallway with a small pail on the floor as she cautiously walked further into the building. Evidently, this home had been empty for quite some time.

She wandered into the only other room and found a bed covered by a Native bed spread. A grimy grey shirt and brown pants were draped over a square wooden box. There was a metal stand up lamp with a blue tattered shade that was almost ready to fall off. Everywhere she walked, the floor boards would crack or creak as though they were going to break at any minute. The place looked eerie.

"This place gives me the creeps. It is as if the owner disappeared into thin air."

It sure needed a lot of attention. Where was the owner? And why did he leave his clothes behind? Looking for clues, Janine went back to the kitchen to see if there were any signs of food eaten or dirty dishes in the sink.

"This, certainly, is a sad way of living. The owner must have been poor. I think that this home once belonged to a Native or someone who likes Native blankets. But why leave behind the pants and shirt. Strange," Janine said.

"What is strange?" asked the mirror.

"Leaving without your pants and shirt and leaving a blanket in the house as if you are not coming back?" Janine frowned.

"Maybe something happened and he was unable to return," the mirror replied.

"So much dust and dirt and look." She opened the tap wide from the spigot to see if any water was available. "No water coming out from the spigot." How can anyone live like this?" she snapped. "Something happened here. I can feel it."

"I think we best leave. There is nothing here anyway. We must stay on track."

"I suppose you are right." She peered between two slats, trying to get a look at the back yard. "There is nothing here. But wait, I see something interesting out there."

"We haven't got time. We must go now. You can look into it later."

Ignoring the mirror, Janine headed for the backyard and studied the deer hide teepee that had been hidden by the house. Native designs of different animals were sewn onto the hide. Janine counted twelve poles, which were straight and smooth, holding up the teepee. They were about one inch thick at the top.

Janine had seen teepees before and knew how the poles worked. Two are for the smoke-vent, which were more slender than the others and had a crosspiece lashed on them about two feet from the top. Janine was drawn to it. She made an attempt to walk around the teepee to see if anyone was inside. She had seen no movement and she couldn't hear anyone. She walked all around it again, studying the intricate work. Now she was curious to see what was inside.

"Janine, don't go in there. You are trespassing into someone else's property," the mirror pleaded.

Ignoring her, Janine opened the flap and quietly ducked inside. "Oh." She was amazed at how big it was. Sunlight beamed through the smoke hole and made the space very bright. Several black bear skins were laid neatly on one side of the teepee. A metal pot hung from a makeshift tripod over a small fire pit in the middle. She went over to see if it was hot. "It is cold, yet; look at this place." Two woven baskets carried pelts and fishing equipment, such as bony hooks and sinew, were neatly stored to one side of the teepee. More metal pots were found on the dirt floor probably for collecting water and used as plates for food.

"Quite a few animal pelts hung around here. Which means that whoever lived here was a hunter and liked this teepee. It is sure better than the old house next to it." Janine was glad to have had the

88

opportunity to view such lodging and hoped not to have to answer to anyone about her trespassing.

"There is no one here." She sighed. "Guess you were right. We should go." Heading back to the road, she took a quick look inside the house again. Still no one, so she walked down the road. Before long, the hair on the back of her neck stood up. An enormous dragonfly shot directly at her.

And before she could run, it snatched her up and flew off.

"Yikes. Let me go!" she screamed.

"I told you to leave at once, but no, you had to explore more and look at what it has got us into," ranted Right Whisper with disgust. "This one looks like it is going to have us as an appetizer."

Fearing for her life, Janine didn't know how long she would be alive because dragonflies immediately decapitate their victims quickly after catching them. Expecting for this large dragonfly to make its move without thought and warning, she was astonished to be surrounded by others. They had obviously gathered to help with the execution.

"Let me go, you big oaf!" she cried.

"Grab your walnuts if you can. You are going to need them," shouted the mirror.

Chapter Fourteen

Corvus sat on a branch of a tree overlooking a dirt road, ready for the encounter that his magical senses had warned him about. He observed its surroundings. And there it was, a black bear lumbering toward him. The crow sensed that he was not in danger due to the bear's body language, but things could change and he was ready.

The bear stopped and looked up at him. "Hello, old friend," the bear said. "It has been a long time since we have met."

"Have I met you before? Don't come any closer or I will have to change my good nature to a wicked one where one of us may be injured."

"That would be sad since I'm not here to hurt you. And besides, I am bigger than you are and it could be serious on your side."

Corvus tilted his head. "You know, your mannerism seems familiar to me and yet you threaten me with your power. Show me your true nature so that I may get a better outline of who you really are." The crow frowned, ready for an assault.

"Not as of yet, my friend." The bear smiled.

"You keep calling me that, but I have yet not placed who you are."

"You are losing your touch, Corvus." The bear moved ever so slowly toward the crow.

"Don't come any closer. I am warning you," the crow said in a shrilling voice.

It was then the bear shook his body and let out a loud growl. He stood up on his hinds and extended his forepaws in the air. He walked backwards a few feet and then stopped. With a loud cry, the bear began to dance and chant, reenacting the ritual of his people by commemorating the power and mystery the earth itself has to offer. He then stopped.

"Oh spirits and guardians of the earth, I thank you for all things Mother Earth has to offer. Please give me strength to save the predecessors of my tribe, my people. I honor you for all that you have done for us: the animal, human, and plant-kind." The bear continued chanting and dancing, a ceremony he was familiar with. All of a sudden an array of psychedelic colors danced around him: blue green, red, yellow etc., which transformed him into a shaman.

"Now do you remember?"

"Well, well, well; it has been a long time." Corvus said. The shaman expressed an amazing fearlessness through his movements. Corvus watched the elder walk up to him. "I was a young bird at the time, but I will always remember you as a dear friend. No tricks, I hope?"

"You were always cautious, Corvus. You realize this place is my home. What trick would I have if I am where I want to be?"

"I have a duty to perform, but I was drawn to fly in this direction and then you show up."

The shaman looked at him and sighed, then gazed down on the grass beside him.

"I may only have one day to live. My life and my people are in grave danger. I need your help."

Corvus knew that the shaman was a magical being, who believed the crow was a spirit animal. He would help his friend if he could. "How can I help? It is your choice as a spiritualist that I am here. So spit it out," insisted the crow. "Where am I going? I do have a duty to perform for Janine."

"My people are important to me and I will stop at nothing to save them. You are my only hope if I am unable to fulfill my responsibility as a leader by tomorrow."

"Only hope to do what?" asked Corvus.

"Save my people from the phantom."

"Aw! You are kidding me, right?"

The shaman stared into the crow's eyes. The air around them shimmered for a moment, and when it had cleared, Corvus could see the shaman's people. He watched as they were transformed into horribly disfigured creatures. When the shaman blinked, the images vanished.

"I had no choice but to follow my people, Corvus. Faeran has granted me a few days to come up with a diversion to keep you away from Janine, but I must save my people."

"Never!" He shook his head. "I will not leave Janine. She is my responsibility. You have yours."

"If you help me, Janine will be spared."

"You realize what you are asking?"

"I was to lure you away long enough for Faeran to seize Janine. Which I believe has already been done. They did not see me since I was transformed as a bear and out of their sight."

"You mean he has her already."

"Yes." The shaman sighed.

"Then tell me, what did you see?"

"He sent huge dragonflies and his guardians to capture her, right here in front of my house not too long ago. I am putting my life in jeopardy sooner than expected. He should be coming for me any minute to dispose of me, but I have a plan. You must not follow me, but follow your instincts. Go through the woods on the southwest side. There you will find a broad cedar path and will be greeted by two chipmunks."

"Two chipmunks? I may have seen them before."

"They will guide you to a small, white mausoleum. On top of the tomb are two concrete, odd gray and black creatures that belong to

Faeran. There you will find a large brown and tanned dragonfly with an oval tan outline on its head. Past its stomach area, is a rusty kind of color with wide tan streaks on its back and tail. Oh, one more thing about him is that, he has piercing, emerald eyes close together. He will be guarding the tomb and will know where Janine is located. You can't miss him. Watch out for him for he is a dangerous predator. Now, leave before danger reaches you," the old native snapped.

"How do you know I will do this for you? I haven't agreed to it yet."

"Stay safe, my friend. I am grateful you are here. Once you have Janine, make your way back to my teepee and the rest will follow. So, please, go and be careful." The shaman shifted into a bear again. Then vanished.

Corvus flew over the house and from the corner of his eye, he could see Faeran's guards trying to invade the shaman's domain, but they couldn't penetrate the electrical current that prevented them from getting close. It was evident the elder was well protected and waited patiently for Corvus's return.

It wasn't long before Corvus finally reached Ci, who was where he'd left him last. The beetle was still sleeping comfortably.

"Wake up, Ci!" the crow yelled. "Wake up!"

"Huh, huh, what is happening? Are the mottled sculpin's back?" The bug rubbed his eyes.

"It's time to move! I think you call it boogey, you know. Can you walk? We haven't much time."

"Go where? What is your hurry?" the bug grumbled.

"How good are you in finding dragonflies?"

"Mmm, one of my favorites."

"How good are you in finding and catching dragonflies?"

"Pretty good, I guess. I am getting hungry after all of this." Ci rubbed his stomach.

"Without swallowing or hurting them?"

"Party pooper. Now that could be tricky, because, of my size." Ci struggled to stand on his feet.

"You will have to do better than that. We have to find Janine and save a friend of mine's people first."

"We have to do what?"

"Save a tribe that belongs to a shaman who was captured by Faeran and made into horrible creatures? He wants them back from the wrath of evil."

"Are you nuts?" Ci snapped. "How do you propose we do that when we ourselves have a mission to complete?"

Corvus flew off. Ci grabbed his walking stick and hobbled after the crow. He fell a couple of times, but recovered.

"Save a tribe," he mumbled. "What tribe? Why now? What about Janine? Come to think of it, no. Not possible." The beetle stopped abruptly and stared around him for a few seconds. "What was I supposed to do?" He shifted his cane. He looked up and caught sight of the crow and said, "Oh, yeah, now I remember."

Chapter Fifteen

"I am hungry," Janine told the big dragonfly who had taken her captive. Several others formed a circle around her. A warm breeze blew across her skin. One of the dragonflies gave her a green leaf.

"A leaf?"

"You said you were hungry. So eat." The big dragonfly chuckled.

"Yes, but a leaf. I am a person not an insect." The big dragonfly smiled.

After she dropped the leaf, she reached into her pocket.

"Don't try to escape because I would hate to see you hurt before…" His voice trailed off and he seemed to have lost interest in their conversation. He watched her silently as she put a few of the walnuts into her mouth and chewed. Before she realized what was happening, the big insect flipped her over into the air and she was tossed roughly from one dragonfly to another. She dropped some of her walnuts on the ground. The insects were laughing and hollering having fun with their prisoner.

"Stop, please!" she cried, but it wasn't until a huge gust of wind blasted across the dirt road that she was thrown onto the ground.

"Ouch!" Her elbow hurt where she'd landed on it, and she rubbed the spot to make it feel better. As she struggled to stand, Faeran strode across the road toward her with his guards. The dragonflies parted to let him through. She stared into his sinister orange eyes and was afraid. She could feel her heartbeat racing so fast, it nearly exploded. She felt like she was going to throw up, but she kept silent and looked around to see if Corvus was nearby. He was not. The few walnuts she ate were not enough to give her the confidence she needed. Silence was in the air, and Janine looked around to see if she could find the missing walnuts.

The phantom folded his arms and tapped his bony, skeletal fingers methodically on his bicep. "Nicely done, Progo." He nodded slightly at the dragonfly and gestured towards Janine.

She watched Faeran closely and noticed he was not affected too much by her state.

"Seize her!" The guards grabbed her. Her heart pounded, but not as badly as it had before. He glided close to her. Then, without a word, his skeletal, right hand went towards her old pouch and pulled out the magical mirror.

"No! Put that back! You have no right, you big bully!" Janine screamed, only to hear the phantom laughing as he tossed the mirror to one of the dragonflies.

"Throw it away. In the lake or the forest. I don't care what you do with it. Just get rid of it. It is of no use to me."

"No, please don't," Janine cried. "I'll do anything you say, but please leave the mirror alone."

He stared at her, before he said, "Very well." He sighed heavily. "I will spare your precious mirror on the condition you come willingly with me without any fuss or muss."

Glaring into his orange, fiery eyes, Janine nodded.

"Well done! Ah, don't be so upset Janine, it isn't all that bad." He turned to his guards. "Take her and don't be so brutal this time." The phantom smiled at her.

"What about the mirror? What are you going to do with it?" she questioned with concern.

"Oh yes, I'll take it with me, just in case you change your mind along the way." He snorted and waved his guards to move along ahead of him. As they were doing so, Faeran signaled the chosen dragonfly he'd asked earlier to dispose of the mirror. "Get rid of it," he whispered. "Give it to the crypt keeper. He'll know what to do with it." The mirror tried to speak but was muffled.

Janine looked back to see if the phantom was near, only to find that he was gliding on the opposite side of her, giving her that wicked smile again. She knew something was up but she wasn't sure what. It made her uneasy. She flipped her hair back and kept her distance from the phantom. She walked a few feet further, but noticed her shoe laces were undone.

"Hold on, my shoe laces are undone." She stopped and bent down to tie her running shoes. As she was bent over, two chipmunks came running up to her. They dropped the rest of the walnuts beside her and continued running past her. She immediately grabbed the walnuts and looked around, hoping no one had seen her. She was right. The guards were not interested in her tying her shoe laces. She hid her walnuts in her pocket.

Even though she was a prisoner, she couldn't help noticing how beautiful the dragonflies were other despite their oversized growth. There were emerald ones, blue ones, sedge color, green ones, blue and green ones, green and brown ones, white, red and yellow tail ones, too. Some had larger heads than others or larger bodies than the rest of them. Quite peculiar that they were all together, but Janine observed each and every one of them kept an eye of what the other dragonfly was doing. As if they were not hundred percent friends. It was clear they were afraid of the phantom and what he might do to them.

As they walked along, Janine hoped that Corvus and Ci would soon be there or able to track her down before Faeran took control of her soul.

Progo was up ahead and Janine decided to have a conversation with him just to find out more information on what their plans were and where she was going.

"What does Progo stand for?" she asked.

The lead dragonfly flew alongside her.

"Progomphus Obcsurus, Latin for my type of breed. And proud of it." He flew back to the head of the line.

"You have such a bright blue body with yellow spots. I love your see-through blue wings. Too bad you're scared of being your own person!" she yelled. Progo promptly fluttered right back to her.

"I am my own person." He glanced quickly at the phantom. "I get to lead all of these dragonflies as my army. If any one of them gets out of line, they will have to stand their ground and fight until one stands no more," he said proudly. "You care to challenge me?"

"Wow! You really believe that or you are obviously controlled to think that way. I know you are a proud insect, but your size is abnormal and you are not in power at all. Faeran is." Someone pushed her abruptly from behind. She turned to find one of the dragonflies buzzing along angrily.

"Stop talking and don't waste our time," he demanded.

"Okay, okay, I'm walking. You don't have to shove. I am sore as it is." She removed the ribbon from her burnt hand carefully. "See, this is what your fellow mates have done to me. Some of the skin came off." She then stuffed her ribbon in her pocket." I need water for my hand."

"Ha, ha," one of the guards burst out and shook his head.

"You fail to recognize that these identities are my protégés," the phantom told her. "And I rule and make it happen. It is up to them to make a choice. As you can see, Miss Janine, they appreciate their positions and fully understand where they stand. You, on the other hand, have to fulfill those obligations and realize what is in store for you. Co-operation, that is all I want. Don't disappoint me, Janine."

"Do I have a choice?" sneered Janine as she looked him right into the eyes.

The phantom just laughed at her as they went through some heavy brush. They came to a rocky section of a mountain where a small entrance was noticeable.

As they got closer, she detected a wooden door where one of the security guards had a key embedded in his left hand. He placed his hand onto the left corner of the door. A light flashed and the door opened.

The guard returned to his post and Janine checked to see if he was any different from the other's garments or identity and all she could detect was a tight, wide, gold choke chain around his neck. Would that be controlled by the phantom as to who comes in or out of the entrance? If that were the case, then consequences would be paid dearly if they were not invited without his knowledge. She spotted the phantom whispering something to the key keeper. Stumbling as she was shoved inside, it wasn't long before she realized she was invisible from the rest of the world. Faeran's prisoner.

She'd never felt so alone and afraid.

A chosen dragonfly stood guard just inside the entry while Progo stood watch by the hallway.

While she wondered what was going to happen to her, dozens of grotesque amphibians crawled toward her, seeming to look her over. Janine was stunned from all of this and did not move an inch as she was surrounded. She put her hands over her eyes and cried. She dropped to the floor, pulled her knees up to her chest and clung onto her knees with her arms as she wept. She was so tired and sore. Then teary eyed and shaking her head, she looked up.

"Welcome," the phantom said to the slithering creatures. "Meet Janine, a newcomer. She will be part of this flock, only she will be my personal serf," he announced with glee.

"I don't know what that means, but I'll bet it indicates personal slave. That is the way it is with you!" cried Janine.

"Whatever. You will serve me and do as I say, whatever I demand." The phantom proudly gazed at his handiwork. "Take her to her quarters, Progo, and take two of my guards with you. Wait there until I arrive. I have some business to attend to first."

Chapter Sixteen

Corvus could not forget what the shaman had previously said. Through his supernatural senses he could hear the elder's spirit speak to him. *Go through the woods on the southwest side of here and you will find a broad cedar path. There you will be greeted by two chipmunks. They will guide you to a small white mausoleum. On top of the tomb are odd gray and black shaped creatures, which are unrecognizable and may belong to Faeran. There you will find a large brown and tanned dragonfly with an oval tan circle on its head and a rusty kind of color past the stomach area, with wide tan streaks on its back and tail that will be guarding it. He is the keeper of the crypt and will know where Janine is located. Oh, one more thing about him is that he has piercing emerald eyes. Watch out for him, for he is a dangerous predator.*

Corvus found the path his shaman friend described and followed it. Periodically, he would check to see if Ci was following him and circled around in the bright blue sky until the insect was in plain view, lying down. He was about to land when, without warning, two chipmunks burst out running from the grass. He immediately fluttered his wings to stay airborne.

They sure looked like the same ones he'd met before, but all chipmunks look the same or do they?

"Are you the chipmunks to guide me to the mausoleum?" asked Corvus.

"Uh-huh, yup," nodded the excited chipmunks. "Whenever you are ready."

"Are you awake Ci?" hollered Corvus to Ci who dozed off.

"I am now," Ci yawned.

"Are you in good form, my friend?" shouted Corvus.

"As well as can be expected from a cripple. Don't mind me, I'll get through it. I know this area quite well." The beetle winced every time he stepped and moving fast was hard on his broken leg. "I'll be available when you need me."

"Are you quite sure?" screeched Corvus while he circled around the insect.

"Quite sure!" Ci hollered back, waving his wooden cane before hastily putting it down to avoid falling. Yes, he does know this area very well. But why? It was as if he been here before, a long time ago. This made him feel uneasy. He couldn't quite pin point what it was, even though he was a fair distance away from the bird.

After about a half hour later, following the chipmunks, Corvus heard some strange noises, like a long inhaling and exhaling sound with a guttural growl. He made a swift dive towards Ci, landing in front of him. The crow made a motion to be very quiet. "Quiet, I hear something," he whispered. Ci turned his head and watched the chipmunks leaving abruptly, which gave Corvus nil time to thank them.

They listened for a few seconds. "Let me check." Corvus flew out of sight. He spotted a dragonfly, and flew back to Ci, who jumped when he landed without warning.

"Ah," Ci cried. "Where did you come from?"

"Shhh. You are not going to like it. The insect is coming toward us. Be prepared for this one, because we must stop this creature to find out where Janine is staying without Faeran noticing anything is wrong. Can you help me?"

"Sure I will help you, but what did you mean by being prepared to meet this one, anyway? Did you mean the dragonfly you spoke about earlier?" questioned the insect.

"Not quite. You will see when it appears in a few minutes, but quick. Hide behind this large bush and catch it when I lure it down your way. Can you do that for me?"

"I'll do my best," Ci answered with hesitation.

"Just make sure you do not harm it in any way," Corvus said in a soft voice.

"I'll try," Ci replied. Before long, the dragonfly flew out from behind a tree, carrying a parcel of some kind. Corvus dive bombed the insect repeatedly. The dragonfly changed courses several times in an effort to escape the crow's attacks, but Corvus was too quick for it. He steered it towards Ci, who managed to grab its tail without killing it. Screaming in pain, the dragonfly twisted and turned frantically in an effort to free itself. It was quite a shocker when Ci noticed the large dragonfly was the same size as he. It was going to be a challenge to keep from hurting it too much.

During the struggle, it dropped the parcel, and Corvus, realizing that it was the rawhide pouch that carried Right Whisper, scooped it up in his beak. This gave Corvus an opening to move the mirror to a safe place.

"Are you all right, Right Whisper?" he quickly asked as he watched Ci holding on to the dragonfly as it struggled to get away.

"Yes, I think so. You must save Janine. She is in grave danger," she replied rapidly.

"I must find out where she is held. Just wait here. I'll be back shortly." Corvus flew straight at the dragonfly, landing on its neck. He dug his talons into its soft tissue, causing it to bleed. It struggled to get free, and Corvus felt he was no match for it, but didn't give up. A few seconds later, the dragonfly began to lose strength.

"Get off of me. You claws are cutting me. I give up!" screeched the dragonfly.

"You only have to co-operate with me and I will let you go," he told it. "But if you fight with me, I cannot guarantee a safe life after this. For, you see, that large insect behind you?"

With difficulty turning its head, the dragonfly nodded.

"On my command, he will chomp down on you, and you, my friend, will lose your tail and eventually die. Is that what you want?" warned the crow as he kept his talons onto the victim's back.

"What do you want with me?" the dragonfly asked.

"Wise choice. I will not remove my claws until you have answered my questions to my satisfaction. And then, I will instruct my friend to let you go, but in return you will tell me where Janine is. Or else you will feel this." He dug his talons a little deeper until he heard the insect cry in agony. Blood dripped between the insect's wings.

"Please, no more," the dragonfly whimpered. "You have made your point. I was instructed to dispose of the mirror for the phantom." It whimpered again. "You are hurting me! I may not be able to fly again if you keep this up!" He tried to lash back at Ci, but failed.

"You still haven't answered my question. Where is she?" Corvus stood on the insect's head and stared at him upside down.

"It is difficult to explain, but I can show you where she is staying, if you prefer," the insect offered, blowing out a noisy breath.

Corvus and Ci exchanged glances. Ci shrugged. The crow decided to give the dragonfly a chance.

"I will accept your offer, but on one condition," Corvus pointed out.

"Oh! What is that?"

The crow leaned over to the dragonfly's face and whispered to him.

"I will remain where I am and my friend will release you, but if you try anything out of the ordinary. I will kill you. You will not see your friends ever again. Do we fully understand each other?"

With great difficulty, the dragonfly nodded and Corvus signaled Ci to release the tail and pick up Right Whisper.

When Ci released him, the dragonfly struggled to lick the blood off his injured neck, warily watching Ci pick up Right Whisper's pouch.

"Get me out of this wrap, Ci. I hate being in the dark," demanded Right Whisper.

"Oh, yes. Sorry."

Ci pulled her out of the pouch and hobbled over to Corvus.

"Are you all right, Right Whisper? Are you damaged in any way?" asked Corvus.

"No, I am fine. Just find Janine, and hurry."

"I am ready, Corvus. You lead on and I will follow. I will not be too far away from you, so don't worry about me. I'll get there sooner or later. Let's not waste any more time, shall we?" Ci insisted.

"Ahhh." With great effort, the flying insect stood up and wasn't sure if it's tail would co-operate in its flight or not. Letting out a huge groan, he said. "Argh! I am grateful that you did not put more pressure on my neck Corvus because I need to see everything, everywhere I go and what is going on. I hope this works." With great effort, he managed to move his neck and tail.

Corvus nudged the dragonfly with his wing. "Move it. Take me to Janine. Now!"

The giant dragonfly glared at Corvus and sluggishly took off into the air. Corvus followed.

"Ci!" Right Whisper yelled.

"What," he answered while he hobbled in a different direction than the one Corvus was headed.

"Where are you going? I thought you were going to follow Corvus. I know where Janine was captured but beyond that, I have no clue where to look. It may save you some time if you follow Corvus up to that point," she cried.

"Great!" He limped back to where he'd started. "What are we waiting for?" Ci leaned on his crutch and stared at her.

"Oh for Pete's sakes, where are you going?" The mirror snapped as she watched Ci struggled with his confusion. The creature was confused so easily and had such a hard time completing a task.

"I am ready for action. Or, maybe not? Time will tell. The way I was headed and the dragonfly going seemed familiar, but I don't know why. If only I can remember…" he said to himself before his voice trailed away.

"Ci. We need to get a move on before Corvus comes back to check on us. Now, let's go!" shouted the mirror.

"I still see him." He grabbed the pouch tightly and off they went.

A crutch on one side of his body and holding the mirror on the other side was not an easy task for the bug and he struggled with every step. Ten minutes later, they arrived shortly after Corvus and the dragonfly landed in front of a thick forest.

"Phew," said Ci who was winded. He set Right Whisper by his side and sat down.

"Let's go," Corvus said.

"Give me a few minutes, old boy."

"No time to waste."

The crow didn't wait and they set off again as Corvus kept a close eye on the dragonfly, which flew somewhat erratically due to its injuries. Before long, it settled on a large flat rock close to a pathway. Hovering over the rock, it turned to Corvus and whispered.

"If you stick to that pathway, you will come to Faeran's secret hideout. I will stay here to rest since, well, I am very sore and this will be a safe place to lick my wounds. You can rest assured I will not go very far with these injuries."

"Just be sure that you know I can catch you faster than you can escape if you cross me," commented Corvus in a soft voice, while he landed between Ci and the dragonfly. The insect nodded. He turned to Ci and Right Whisper.

"Let's not waste any time," whispered Corvus. He flew close to the ground towards Faeran's lair. With enormous caution, Corvus was up ahead and the other two moved slowly down the path before they spotted an unexpected guard. Hovering on the path was a dragonfly that was larger than the one they'd injured. They stopped and threw themselves into a nearby bush.

"Where did he come from?" Ci whispered to the mirror.

"He must be the keeper of the mausoleum, and no one is going to get past him, if he can help it," she pointed out. "You best think of a plan or we will be here for a very long, long, time."

"How did you know about this, Right Whisper?" asked Corvus.

"I heard Faeran speak to the dragonfly who took me."

"Shh! Let me think what our next move will be, you two," the crow insisted. He peered at the dragonfly from the bushes and wondered if this was the dragonfly the shaman had warned him about. The giant was much larger than the injured dragonfly and he wasn't sure if Ci's mouth which still hung open in surprise, was large enough to catch it.

"Not a sound." Corvus swung his right wing across Ci's mouth to shut it. "You can slam your choppers now. It won't go away. We have got to come up with a plan and fast. The crypt must be close by," muttered the crow. "Yet, there's something about this particular bug. I can't just place it. Right Whisper, there is something familiar with this one. Can you help me?"

Ci placed the mirror where she could study the dragonfly. She motioned Corvus towards her and whispered in his ear. He then looked at the large bug and bobbed his head slowly in agreement.

"Of course. Now I know."

"Know what?" interrupted Ci as he hovered over his colleagues catching them by surprise.

"Ahh. I hate when you do that," said the crow.

"Do what?"

"Creep up on us."

"Sorry, force of habit. So, what is our next move?"

Corvus gradually looked up and smiled at Ci. "You, my man, will be his bait. You are injured and he may go for it. Are you bug enough to do it?"

Dumbfounded, Ci sputtered, "Bait? Bug enough. Ha! ha! Very funny." There was, a moment of silence. "Are you serious? Did you hit your head recently or have a bad fall? Because I don't recall electing myself to be in someone else's food chain. Have you seen the size of…whatever it is…that thing? That…that thing is way over my head. Literally. That's a bad idea."

"We know you can do it. I am sure you have faced other challenges in the past," assured the crow.

"Serious? Um, I am not sure I can do this. This whole idea is ludicrous," said Ci. "I think the element of surprise is a better one."

Corvus knew there were limits to this situation and Ci would certainly be in danger, but help with this issue from the mirror may just work. It was a risk he had to take. They needed to subdue the dragonfly because, once he was, they could convince the monster that it had other alternatives to choose from other than being attracted to live bait and being Faeran's crypt keeper.

"You know, you are right, Ci. It is a ridiculous plan. We will have to find another way to save Janine, but we may be too late since Faeran has had her for some time now," explained Corvus.

With a big sigh, he mumbled, *"'Why can't I come up with better suggestions at a spur of a moment like Corvus'."* Ci hobbled across the path with Right Whisper in hand. He stopped in front of the giant dragonfly. It did not take long before the giant keeper spotted him and immediately pursued its target.

"You there! What are you doing here? What is your purpose?" hollered the flying insect.

"Who, me?" Ci smiled broadly and in a squeaky voice he said, "Is this not the way to… Now, wait a minute. Let me think. I must have gone north instead of south to meet my cousin." Ci hobbled as he continued to mumble. Losing patience, the monster was ready to attack and it sized Ci up with its huge emerald eyes.

"Careful, Ci. They have great vision. He can probably see Corvus and me," whispered Right Whisper.

The dragonfly's wings were in motion independently and flew with great speed, shifting its direction with ease, like a helicopter. Ci watched it closely as the dragonfly flew toward him from behind.

"Look out Ci!" screamed the mirror. Ci ducked, but could see the serrated jaw as it opened its mouth.

"Oh my gosh!" shrieked Ci. "He's coming back."

"Are you ready, Right Whisper? Because this is going to be the only attack I am allowed before he bites my head off."

"With my special powers, I hope this works because their eyesight can reduce the sun's glare when over water, like sunglasses. I have to be dead on. The element of surprise on dry land."

With great speed, the dragonfly flew sideways before it shifted its great wings and flew straight at them. Without warning, the dragonfly was blinded by a bright light from the mirror. It fell to the ground with a thump, while the mirror directed the light straight at the insect. The dragonfly thrashed violently, shaking its head and trying to avoid the light. But no matter which way it twisted, it could not get away from the beam of light. It was like a magnet.

"Careful, Ci. Don't go near it until the dragonfly surrenders. I don't know how long my powers can last to keep it from attacking us."

"Grrr." The dragonfly shook its head several times, trying to avoid looking at the mirror, but the light was too strong. It paralyzed him to the point that he was unable to focus on his target. "Point that light somewhere else," he demanded.

He failed at every turn. He could not gain his stance nor protect the mausoleum from these intruders. He felt helpless. Right Whisper faced the giant dragonfly with Ci's help and rearranged herself for her next step.

"Rusty," she said.

"Why are you calling me Rusty?" the insect asked. "I don't know you and you are trespassing."

"I want to show you something."

"I'm not interested."

"Rusty. Listen to me. We are not here to hurt you. We just want you to understand something. I want you to see something beautiful about yourself and how handsome you once were. Can you give me that chance?"

"I know who I am. I am the keeper of the mausoleum. And when I am finished with you, I won't need to listen to your nonsensical illusion of who I am," he answered with great pride.

"Do you remember a little girl named Janine, who was on the dock one day and named you Rusty? She told you how stunning you were just before Faeran took hold of you." The dragonfly shook his head.

The powerful light dimmed, and the dragonfly slowed his struggles. An image appeared within the mirror that drew its attention. It was a young dragonfly with a rust colored stomach.

"Remember this?" Right Whisper asked. "That was you. Look how magnificent you were. And let me show you how you look now." The image disappeared, and the dragonfly saw its own reflection. "Which one do you prefer?"

"Hello, Rusty." He jumped in surprise when Corvus landed on the back of his neck and he shook his head forcefully.

"What do you plan to do with me? I see that you have great powers, probably as powerful as Faeran's supernatural abilities."

"As I said before, we are not here to hurt you."

"So why is the crow on the back of my neck, if you are not here to hurt me?"

"Leverage, in case you decide to turn against us," answered Corvus. "I've had practice." The dragonfly turned his head and stared at the crow.

"What do you want from me?" Rusty moaned. "You are trespassing and if you are caught, there will be consequences to pay."

"Oh, really? Funny, since you are at risk with me. Wouldn't you say?" Corvus planted himself firmly on the dragonfly's neck.

"Faeran will be here any minute now and he will know what to do with you. You cannot escape or hide from him." Rusty snickered.

"That is just it. Faeran is too busy with other things and trusts you to protect this area. He doesn't know we are here." The crow tilted his head at the dragonfly. "Neither of us is afraid of him and certainly, with your size at hand, he needs you here to protect his domain. So you see, he has no reason to check on you since you are his prized possession and creation." Corvus glanced at Right Whisper and gestured for her to proceed with the plan.

She nodded and turned to Rusty. "Focus, Rusty. Look into the mirror."

"What are you going to do to me? Hypnotize me?" he asked.

"No. I am not going to hypnotize you, but I will need your attention. There is a goal I wish you to go for. You need to concentrate on your future and not be fixed on being just a huge blimp and a keeper. There is more to life than…this." Right Whisper positioned herself on Ci's back. "Take a good look at this image." Rusty moved closer to her. He peered into the mirror.

Images of normal dragonflies hatching from their larvae before they frolicked in the warm spring air and tested their fresh wings reflected from the glass. They were having fun and enjoying their new bodies. He closed his eyes for a moment and then looked again at Right Whisper.

"Is this true? Do they really live like this?"

"We want to give you a second chance, Rusty. A chance to live a normal life rather than be Faeran's pawn."

He looked at her skeptically. "How do I know this is not a trick? How do I know that you won't be the same as Faeran? Doing just what he did to me as you called it, made me his pawn."

"Trust. I…we are not lying to you. It's the truth. Janine is being kept captive here and we are at a point where we need to rescue her from Faeran. We need your help." Corvus smiled at Rusty while he looked at his opponent upside down.

"She is not here! Faeran assured me that there were no prisoners in his cells. He did not come through here. I have been here all day. So you are all full of baloney. Besides my name is Snaketail, not Rusty."

"That makes sense. Anyway, that is where you are wrong, Rusty. She is in there for sure. We bet our lives on that," Ci said.

"Is there another way of getting into the mausoleum?" asked Corvus.

"Yes, the other side of the mausoleum. Faeran or the key keeper would have told me. So I would know if she went through that way."

"Maybe they didn't tell you this time," said the mirror.

"They would have told me. I'll tell you what. If she is there, I will help you get her out, but if she isn't, well…life will be quite different for all of you. If you get my meaning?" said Rusty wryly.

Corvus nodded. "Okay. Deal."

"What?" questioned the other two.

"Are you nuts?" Ci exclaimed. "We will get killed in there. You know what; you did hit your head on something, because you are not thinking straight, my man. I trusted you until just now, but I am not going in there. Besides, Faeran is waiting to catch me. Dead, right. You are off your rocker." Ci shook his head and turned to walk away.

"Get back here Ci, I am not done." Ci stopped and hobbled back at the crow's words. "Hear me out guys. It is a sure thing the phantom cannot catch me because he has nothing on me, but you he wants. Especially, you, Ci. So if Rusty brings you two as prisoners, Faeran will be pleased. Right?" commented Corvus.

"He will think something's up, and besides, where will you be, since we are bait?" questioned Ci.

"I'll be around. Don't you worry," the crow replied.

"I am worried, but it isn't going to do me any good, is it?"

"Nope. Now let's not dilly dally. Shall we proceed?"

"Where will you be if we need you?" questioned the mirror.

"I am staying right where I am. Aren't I, Rusty?" said the crow. "Right underneath the rawhide cloak you wore earlier."

They all smiled except for the dragonfly. Off they went to the crypt.

Chapter Seventeen

The phantom gathered his prized guards and was about to leave to one of his chambers when Rusty entered unexpectedly. "Why have you abandoned your post?" Faeran demanded.

"Look what I found sneaking around the area with the mirror in hand," the dragonfly told him.

"What have we here?" He floated towards Rusty and his prisoners. "This is getting better than I thought. Guards! Seize them and give me the mirror. What a surprise. Well, isn't this delightful. Quite unexpected, but delightful. Um, I wonder how the mirror ended up with you Snaketail? You were to destroy it. No matter, I have just the place for you two." At that moment, the responsible injured dragonfly who'd had the mirror hid in one of Faeran's chambers, and peered around the corner to see what was happening with the prisoners.

"You have done well, Snaketail, but, first, I must see someone."

"Ci and the mirror are the only prisoners here, right?" asked Rusty.

The phantom turned his head slightly and quickly glided towards the injured dragonfly without warning, who was hiding. At that point, Rusty quietly let Corvus in.

"I gave you one simple task and you can't even follow instructions. Why does Snaketail have the mirror and not destroy it? What good are you?"

"Give me a chance to explain, your Excellency, you see…" cried the injured dragonfly.

"Oh, please. Why were you hiding? Look at the size of you and look at them. What does that tell me? You are incompetent. I see you as damaged goods. You are of no use to me."

"Please, have mercy on me!" Faeran pointed his finger at him. Flames shot out and torched it. The dragonfly screamed with agony until it was nothing but dust. "That feels better. Can't be too sure these days." The creatures and dragonflies were disheartened at what they just saw. The phantom glided back to Ci with the mirror in hand. "Ci, so good of you to drop in." Faeran blew on his finger, mimicking a gunslinger blowing the smoke from his pistol sway. "You were one of my favorites. What happened back there? We had a deal and I trusted you. Did you think that you could escape from me?" smiled Faeran.

"Oh, you mean when I was supposed to hand Janine back to you from the magic tree? Is that what you mean?"

"Hmm. I am surprised at you, but one must move on. I am surprised you remembered all that. I will have to work on you later. Make you perform your tasks better. Take the mirror and him to the cells." The guards grabbed the two and dragged the bug roughly as they ignored his sore leg. "Not you, Snaketail. You go back to your duties. Meanwhile, I have to attend to another matter." He rushed out with his special guards and Progo.

One of Faeran's guards pushed Ci, who fell hard on his injured leg.

"Ow! Watch it," he cried.

While the guard's attention was focused on Ci, Corvus and Rusty attacked the guards from behind, knocking them down by pushing them against the wall. Rusty grabbed Ci and Corvus rescued the mirror.

"Hurry!" Corvus flew down a corridor. "This way." They found Janine two cells down.

"He lied to me. He told me that no one was imprisoned here when in fact there was," remarked Rusty. He looked so disappointed.

"Rusty, is that you? I thought I would never see you. How?" asked Janine as she examined him carefully. Corvus handed Right Whisper to Janine.

"We will explain later, but right now, it is time to rescue the shaman's people and save the forest," Corvus urged. "I have a sneaky suspicion that Faeran is not coming back because he is off to destroy more forests. We have no idea where he went."

"How are we going to free these creatures?" asked Janine.

"They are actually people, not creatures." Corvus hopped to the cell door and glanced down the corridor.

"They are?" She popped a few walnuts into her mouth to calm her nerves. "You are staying with me, Right Whisper." She quickly placed the mirror in her pouch.

Corvus nodded. "They are the shaman's tribe. We have to help them."

"Have any ideas what to do next, Corvus?" asked Rusty, who was balancing Ci and struggling to stay upright.

"Yes, I do and I will need your assistance."

"My role is done here. Just say the word," remarked Rusty.

"Follow my lead and you do the rest on cue," exclaimed the crow, who flew at once to the main room where most of the creatures were present. Some of Faeran's guards were surprised to see the prisoners and tried to apprehend them, but were soon overtaken when Rusty let go of Ci, and helped the crow. Janine's quick reflexes caught the beetle before he fell and she pulled him into the corner where they could hide.

The dragonfly flew with extreme speed using his independent wings to confuse the guards as to which direction he was coming from. They were knocked down and grabbed by his serrated jaws where he dismembered them. Corvus used his talons to transport them to the nearby cells, and defended himself using his beak and talons if need be. Soon, the remaining guards surrendered. Rusty, since he was the strongest and largest dragonfly, escorted them to the cells. Making their way back to the main room, they noticed all of the creatures did not move.

"We are not here to harm you," Corvus told them, "but to recover your true identity. You will need to be assured that we mean no harm to any of you, provided you recover your identity and gain confidence in yourself. Are you willing to fight for your freedom? I realize you are afraid of Snaketail, but I swear to you, he will not hurt you in any way. We have imprisoned the guards in the cells."

There was silence for a moment before one of the creatures slithered over to the cells, then returned moments later.

"We have been tricked before," it said. "And look what happened to us."

"We are telling you the truth," Janine said as she came out from hiding. "We are leaving shortly, and if you wish to follow and become your true self, you are welcome."

"Well? What will it be? Prisoner or freedom?" the crow shouted. Not a creature moved.

"It's too late for me," said Rusty. "But it's not too late for you."

Without another word, Corvus motioned his team to leave the chamber.

"Well Corvus, you tried. I guess they decided to stay here," said Janine as they walked out of the mausoleum.

It was then one of the slithering creatures spoke up. "If we stay the way we are, we have failed as a people, and Faeran has won. I'd rather take my chances out there than rot in here. Who will teach our children our ways? We are a proud nation. We have paid with sorrow and pain. We must prosper in all things where he cannot proclaim our cultural worth. We must preserve it with what is left from the days of our ancestors. Faeran has already destroyed one of our elders. We must protect the other elder, who is a living memory of our ancestors. We must preserve those values and each other. We must stay strong and become proud people we once were. We must fight for our freedom. Who is with me?" The slithering creature began to leave the chamber and turned to say, "I am leaving now with or without you."

Without another word, all of the creatures followed. As they left the confines of the chamber, they transformed into their former selves.

"Hooray! Yahoo!" They yelled with happiness and joy as they felt their bodies return.

Rusty, Janine, Ci and Corvus turned around and were surprised at what they saw, but were happy to see the smiles and comradery that transpired in front of them. "You realize Faeran will feel some pain in his body due to the lack of their souls in his possession," said the mirror to Janine.

"Yes, I know. He will be weaker in his powers to control our fears."

"I am glad to see you all before me. But wait just a minute," Rusty said, and disappeared into the chamber. When he came back he said, "Just as I thought."

"Thought what?" asked Corvus.

"The golden key keeper is gone," answered the dragonfly.

"I thought so. He was the only one that had it on him, because all the other guards did not have a key carved in their hand," said Janine.

"We must hurry to see the shaman. That is where Faeran is headed, and he will use the security guard as his leverage," said Rusty.

"Smart and hope you are right," uttered Corvus.

"We will have to be smarter," retorted Rusty.

Ci, with the help of a tall native, led most of the people toward the old house of the shaman, while Rusty carried Janine on his back toward the indigenous teepee. Corvus took the same route. Within fifteen minutes, they reached their destination only to find Faeran, the security guard and his followers surrounding the shaman's teepee.

"Oh, my goodness! We have visitors. I thought you might pop by Snaketail. A sucker for young Janine. Never got over it, did you?" said Faeran. He tried to hide a wince, but they all saw that he was in pain.

"It's working, Janine," whispered Right Whisper.

"I know."

"You lied to me, Faeran. You did put her in prison," blurted Rusty.

"Just a little white lie. You didn't think I would let her slip through my fingers, did you?" The phantom leaned forward holding his stomach, and then tried to smile.

"What's wrong Faeran. Are you in pain?" Janine asked.

"Nonsense. Just a minor intrusion that can be fixed. Right boys?" He looked back at his guards, who all snickered.

"You will leave these premises and never come back. Leave us alone to live our normal lives," Rusty said.

"I don't think so. For, you see, I hold the key." The phantom sneered. "Shaman, you have but a few seconds until I give the guard the go ahead to destroy another forest, which, in fact, will bring me more power than ever before!"

"Over my dead body," Rusty exclaimed. "I will challenge any one of your dragonflies for the safety of the forest. And if I lose, well then you have the upper hand." He then dropped Janine and the mirror on the ground away from Faeran, before he returned to face the phantom.

"Me too, Faeran. You know I do not fear you and that is why you are afraid of me. You cannot control my soul. You grow on others through their fear. It's over. Your guards are in prison and cannot help you, and you are outnumbered at the moment." The phantom had a hard time moving, but stayed a fair distance away from Corvus.

"This is my fight Corvus. Whatever happens," Rusty whispered. "You are to lure the guard towards the teepee and Janine, you and him are to enter the teepee as fast as you can, no matter what. That is my wish. Is that understood?" The crow nodded reluctantly.

"I accept your contest." The phantom snickered again. "I always love aggravations, don't you? I can choose whoever I want to take you down, Snaketail. I have a well-trained opponent for this very occasion." He turned to the dragonfly. "Progo! Will you please step up to the plate!" exclaimed Faeran and then asked a guard to hold him steady.

"No!" yelled Janine. "You can't do that!"

"I can and I will," boasted the phantom. "This is going to be fun to watch." He again felt a stronger pain on his side this time. "Pick a spot and Progo will follow. May the best dragonfly be my devotee."

"Be ready, Corvus. And Janine, don't look back," whispered Rusty as he chose his spot for sparring.

It did not take long before each dragonfly flung at the other's head to tear a chunk off. Progo was nicked on the side of his head and managed to escape from Rusty's counter attack. Janine noticed blood dripping from the back of Rusty's neck. Instinctively, she got in the way of the battle when Rusty swished his tail toward her and the golden key keeper, and flung them to the other end of the area. This, of course, amused the phantom and his friends, when in fact it was a ploy to get Janine and the guard into the tent. Corvus pushed them in.

As the fight went on, Faeran was surrounded by the strong souls of Aboriginals who had escaped from his prison. He could not control them, and Faeran began to fade. His orange eyes glowed with hatred.

"This isn't over yet!" he cried. The phantom, his guards and Progo vanished. They left Rusty severely injured and were not prepared to help him.

Corvus flew immediately to Rusty. "Janine was right. You are magnificent. Against all odds, you have demonstrated remarkable strength and endurance, more than one could ever ask of you. You will not be forgotten, my friend. You can rest now. Live in peace and tranquility. I will stay with you. You will not die alone." A tear fell from Rusty's eye.

"Tell Janine that my spirit will always be with her."

Then he drew his last breath.

Chapter Eighteen

Inside the teepee, Janine stood quietly while the shaman chanted. He held on to a carved wooden staff decorated with beautiful bird feathers. The key keeper tried to escape, but whenever he touched the hide of the teepee, it felt like a brick wall.

"Get me out of here!" he yelled and tried everywhere in the tent to break away, but failed. Frightened from his imprisonment, the key keeper ran to attack the shaman, but was quickly apprehended by the old aboriginal who used his staff and tripped him.

"Sit by the fire, stay still and pay attention." The key keeper slowly got up as he bared his teeth but he sat by the fire instead of attacking. Janine watched all this with interest, but felt sad knowing Rusty was out there defending himself to save her. She was beginning to get quite fatigued and sat down by the edge of the tent to watch the shaman.

His chanting was loud and his calls to the spirits were convincing and sincere. A fire blazed in the center of the teepee near where the imprisoned key keeper sat. The shaman threw some grey powder into the fire, sending off a despicable odor. He watched his hostage closely until the key keeper looked like he was drugged. Soon after, the shaman placed the key keeper's left arm onto his staff causing the captive to scream with pain. The staff shimmered and transformed into a tall grey maple tree with a large pointy head. The shaman spoke to it in his native tongue and the tree nodded its head. The key keeper fainted.

"It is done," the shaman whispered and the tree disappeared. Right after, the elder stamped his staff onto the ground and a "Whoosh" sound came and went. Corvus entered the tent.

"All is well, my friend?" he asked the elder with excitement.

"Yes. The forest has been saved and so have my people." The shaman smiled at the crow. "Miigwech, Corvus."

"You are welcome. For now, you are at ease. You longed for this day to come. Faeran has finally left, but I have a feeling he will be back with a full vengeance," answered the black crow. "But for the moment, we will enjoy our lives without his wrath. What about him?" The crow gestured at the sleeping key keeper. "What are you going to do with him?"

"Nothing. He is free to go, but he is aware of his identity now and if he returns to Faeran, he will not be so lucky," the shaman said. "The shield is discharged and you are now safe to continue with your journey. Take two of my strong men with you and get Janine to a place where she can rest. She is getting very tired now. Right Whisper will tell you where to go."

"Yes, I have noticed," answered the crow.

"Goodbye, my friend, and be well." The shaman walked over to Janine. "You must leave now so I may prepare a happy festive ceremony for my people. We have a lot to do with our new freedom. Go with peace in your heart and embrace your young soul with love and new frontier wherever your path will lead you."

"Thank you. Corvus, what about Rusty?" asked Janine.

The crow shook his head. "He was a brave soul. He did what was right Janine. I stayed with him to the very end. He will not be forgotten. He did tell me that his spirit will always be with you."

120

Janine cried and cried until she was too exhausted to continue. The crow put his wings around her.

The shaman returned to the flaming fire pit and carried on with his chant. Two young muscular men entered and transported Janine out of the tent. There she saw Rusty lying peacefully.

"Take me to him." The young men did what they were instructed to do. She knelt beside the dragonfly and caressed him. "Thank you for saving my life, Rusty. You will be in my heart forever." She had tears in her eyes. She then handed Right Whisper to one of the young men and they promptly took her up to the nearby hill across the dirt road to the spot where Janine first saw the old boarded-up house.

There they placed her gently on some soft grass and bowed to her as they left. *Why did they behave that way,* she wondered. And why had she, for a split second, felt it was normal? It was peculiar.

At any rate, she felt relieved that all had gone well. Right now she was at a safe place and where she wanted to be. Corvus was by her side and so was the mirror. She had just started to relax when she spied two figures heading her way. One was a tall, middle aged Aboriginal man wearing buckskin leggings, moccasins and a red checkered cotton shirt. Next to him walked a limping grey wolf. She looked at Corvus and Right Whisper, who did not seem surprised to see the two strangers. In fact, they seemed pleased and delighted. Then two young children approached giggling and chasing one another until the middle aged Aboriginal man told them to be quiet.

"Finally, Janine, it is at long last but great to meet you," the man said. "You look rather puzzled as to who we are. I can assure you that we have met before, but under different circumstances. Not most pleasant, I can say, but we have met before."

Baffled by the stranger's comments and their identity, she nevertheless stood up to greet them properly. "I am sorry to tell you, but I don't remember ever meeting you. Maybe Corvus or Right Whisper, but not me."

"Sure you have. Just in a different form, Janine. That's all," the mirror said in a low voice.

"When did I ever see these people, Right Whisper?" asked Janine, confused.

"In the beginning," answered the mirror.

"In the beginning? In the beginning, we were greeted by a huge snapper whose name was Tina. Even Corvus can swear to that. Can't you, Corvus?"

"Yes, yes, but, I found out who Tina really was, from one of the warriors down below, just before I entered the tent."

"Ohhh, ohhh my. Then everything changed once the shaman chanted. So who are you, then?" she asked.

"I am Chief Strong Wolf and this is my best four legged friend, Canis Lupus, or Ci as you know him," replied the man. "And these children are also mine, Achachak and Alsoomse. They were the two chipmunks. The two spies."

Janine's mouth dropped. She was at a loss for words. She fell onto her knees and caressed the wolf. "You are a remarkable creature," she said. "Thank you for saving my life back there in the tunnel. But I do have to ask, why were you both separated from each other and placed with two different identities?"

"Faeran. He decided to teach me a lesson as to be an absented minded buffoon so that I would forget who I was, but I played his game to the fullest. I was glad you came along so that I could use you as my bait. Once I was in the magical tree, the phantom was unable to touch me and with the help of Corvus, I was able to continue on with my own mission," the wolf answered telepathically.

Janine hugged the animal, and boasted, "We sure taught him a lesson or two that you don't mess with the strong, dedicated and passionate people, because we can be so helpful with one another." She began to feel dizzy. "Oh, I don't feel so good. Right Whisper, Corvus, I…I." She lay down on the grass. "I have but one question. I had a dream where I saw happy, lively native people down below and that I was part of them. It felt as if it was family to me. How come I felt that way and why did the natives bow to me?"

"We all have some spiritual powers. You happen to tune in on it. Legend says that a chief's young daughter lost her family and tribe due to a fire, but was saved by a four legged creature and disappeared. No one has ever seen her again. This was centuries ago and maybe you have tapped in on it. Only you will know the truth." Janine sighed and looked at Ci who winked at her.

"Sleep well my little one," Corvus whispered, "for Right Whisper and I will see you again. I won't be far away. Be brave when you wake up in your world."

****

"Janine, Janine, can you hear me?" Someone was shaking her roughly. "Janine, your parents and sister will be here any moment now. Janine, wake up." said the property owner of the barn. Janine opened her eyes slowly and saw the woman kneeling beside her in the living room of the house.

"What happened? Where am I?" Janine sat up and felt her back. "My back hurts. And why is there blood on your hands?" cried Janine.

"You were bitten by my pony, Sam. He was led too close to you and he decided to bite you. He does not like to be led without seeing where he's going, so he..."

"He bit me? How bad is it?" Janine asked nervously.

"You'll live. He left you with some teeth marks. I patted some rubbing alcohol on your back and in a few days the swelling will drop. Have your parents keep an eye on it so that it does not get infected. Oh! Here they are now."

"Maman, Papa, Elisabeth. Am I ever glad to see you! I am all right. I just have to be brave." From the corner of her eye, she happened to see a crow perched on the owner's fence cawing and nodding its head.

The End for now.

Acknowledgements

I would like to thank the following people for their invaluable help with my book: Jana Rade (Book Cover Design), Sirena Van Schaik (Editor) and Kitty Honeycutt (Publisher).

About the Author

Joëlle Hübner-McLean was born in Nancy, France and landed as an immigrant with her parents at Pier 21 Nova Scotia, Canada in the 50's. Married to a wonderful man, with 2 sons and two grandsons, she holds her life with her family dear to her heart. She graduated from Trent University, Peterborough, Ontario in Cultural/Native Studies with a Bachelor of Arts (Hon.) in 2002; Bachelor of Education from York University, Toronto, Ontario in 2003 and Additional qualifications as a Special Education, Specialist in 2007.

Hübner-McLean enjoys music, gardening, animals and birds, walking in the woods and boating. Her passion is writing plays, non-fiction and fiction stories and historical issues. Presently, lives in the outskirts of Perth, Ontario and retired from teaching from the York Region District School Board teaching Secondary level students grade 9-12 Learning Strategies, History, Geography and Applied English.

March 14/13 she was on Rogers TVO/Daytime in Ottawa to promote this book and its up-coming series as well. As a published author for a local newspaper, Coaststar in St. Augustine, Quebec, Labrador, Newfoundland and Ottawa; published author for the website, www.wildviolet.net/birthday_blue/leon.html or on her website: www.corvusandme.com. She was also recognized by the Women's Status of Canada in 2002 due to the above journal. Recognized member of Worldwide Who's Who Branding. Part of the Writer's Festival of Ottawa, August 23, 2014. Now member of the Retired Women of Teaching of Ontario (RWTO) 2015.

Joëlle now retired was a Secondary teacher in Special Education and English so that she could give her students a chance to express themselves and create their own identity. For she knew how to tune in what children face day to day of their lives and tries to maintain the importance of that fact in her stories where kids can relate. Even though Hübner-McLean's book is geared for young adults, its reminiscent prose and settings would appeal to the older audience as well.

Made in the USA
Columbia, SC
10 August 2017